A
Mutually
Beneficial
Arrangement

D1714521

Christina C. Jones
warm hues creative.

One.

Be a good sport, Rowan.

I repeated those words over in my head as I forced a smile to my face, blinking back tears as I offered my opponent their deserved applause. They'd put in work just like I had, had sacrificed time and energy to earn today's prize.

It wasn't fair, but it *was.*

I couldn't be mad, but I *was.*

I should be happy for them, but I wasn't.

As I watched the winners jump up from their table, hugging and shouting and crying over the results, I willed myself to find the good in defeat.

I failed.

It wasn't that I had anything against the *Irving Initiative* – they did great, necessary work toward rehabilitating former felons. Clearing records for non-violent crimes, restoring voting rights, career help, all sorts of things.

But.

In a world where both charity dollars and public funding were limited, the fact that *they* had just been chosen as the recipients of the grant I'd busted my ass applying for made me sick to my stomach. Unfortunately, it was a disappointment I would have to swallow, since I had a young colleague beside me who needed me to set a good example.

After I'd clapped for an appropriate length, I turned to Mila. Her eyes were wet, because she knew the gravity of this decision – knew what it meant for us.

"You'd better not," I whispered to her, looking her dead in the face as she sucked in a breath. "Not right now. Some of the kids came. Not in front of them."

I hated to be harsh with her, but it was necessary. The kids sprinkled into the audience of this town-hall style meeting were just a few of the many served by the Cartwright Center. If they saw us looking defeated, that energy would spread quickly, and that was the last thing we needed. As much as I wanted to scream, cry, throw myself on the floor and beg, I knew how important it was to present a face of hope to those kids.

For many of them, it was the only positivity they saw.

The next hour passed in a blur of handshakes and maybe-next-times, and then I found myself locked in my too-small, too-hot, too-old office until well past the time the center closed, crunching numbers in an attempt to make them work. The thing about budgets though was that required money, and money was something we sorely lacked.

State funding had been cut to the bare minimum – so much that the only salary I took was just enough to pay my necessary bills. That was something I had in common with the center – only the *absolute* necessities. Every other penny, I made sure it was sowed into these kids.

But now… we were out of pennies too.

I drummed my fingers on the top of the rickety, rusty desk, not wanting to hit the "submit" button on my screen that would send the funds to pay the center's electricity bill. Once I did it, we'd have a whopping twelve dollars and sixty-one cents in the account, and I… *God* I didn't want to press that button, but I knew the bright red *final notice* envelope buried within the stack of bills in the tray was no idle threat.

They would *really* cut this shit off.

I bit back fresh tears as I submitted the bill and then flipped the lid of my laptop closed, ready to finally call it a night. As I packed my things away, I wondered if I could talk the vendors who were donating snacks for our upcoming softball game into giving *just* a little more... we could use the extra to feed hungry kids in the coming weeks before another check came in.

Making a mental note to practice my puppy-dog eyes and begging voice, I hung my bag over my shoulder and headed out, shutting everything down as I went. My eyes traveled over chipped and missing tiles, stained chairs, broken mirrors, shoddy air-conditioning, malfunctioning electronics – a whole, *long* list of flaws that, the day before, I'd had real hope of correcting. Because I had good people on board, we managed to keep the place clean, and safe – the least we could do to help give these kids a sanctuary. It cost us nothing except a little elbow grease.

New tiles, fresh upholstery, a contractor, renovated HVAC and an updated computer lab though... *money*.

It always came down to money.

I pulled the door closed behind me with a sigh, knowing I wasn't going home to do anything that even resembled "rest". I'd be digging through financial records, trying to find past donors who hadn't slid anything our way in a while, hoping they'd appreciate a check-in – and show that appreciation with a check.

I was *not* too proud to beg.

In fact, I was so worn down, so desperate, that the thought didn't even make me ashamed – it was just something I would have to do. This was *Vegas*! No, it wasn't all bright lights and casinos like the stereotype said, but there were enough people here with money that surely *someone* was feeling generous?

The night was cooler than I'd expected – too cool for me to be in just a thin button-up underneath my *Cartwright Center*

8

tee shirt. I wrapped my arms around myself as I headed up the nearly-empty sidewalk, grateful that the busted streetlight had been fixed, so at least I wasn't walking home alone in complete darkness.

I waved to a couple of older boys I knew. Boys who'd aged out of the center, but who we'd impacted enough that – even though they hadn't gotten as far away from the streets as I'd hoped – they used whatever little clout they had to make sure the center was left alone. Nobody broke through the flimsy locks to steal the outdated computers, nobody was dealing anything on our playground or the sidewalk directly in front of us.

It was those small favors that added up.

As I turned the corner to my apartment complex, a chill that had nothing to do with the weather crept up my spine. A glance behind me showed two mean-looking women in black suits that were way too nice for around here, and a black SUV that was noticeably luxurious too, creeping down the street.

What the hell is going on?

I started moving a little faster, and slipped my hand into my bag for my phone. I put my finger on the power button, knowing if I tapped it fast enough, multiple times, the safety feature would trigger an emergency call. I had no idea what was happening, but I *did* know that I didn't want to be around for it. I didn't breathe easy until I was in my building, up the elevator, and locked securely behind my apartment door.

Leaving the lights off, I went to my window and peeked out, onto the street. The women and the SUV were still there, but it was parked now, and the women weren't looking at my building.

Good.

Feeling a little better, I dropped my bag onto the couch and then moved to my refrigerator, pulling it open. Immediately, my nose wrinkled as I surveyed the contents, or lack thereof. I couldn't remember the last time I'd ordered Chinese takeout and yet there it was, in greasy, soggy containers. A package of sliced cheese. A jar of... pickles? A shriveled orange. Two bottles of cold-brew coffee. And an already opened, screw-top bottle of Moscato, age unknown.

I shrugged.

"Wine for dinner it is," I muttered to myself, grabbing it and pushing the door closed before I headed back to the couch, not bothering to get a glass. I flipped the TV on and started up Netflix, my one indulgence, since paying for cable was out of the question.

With my computer in my lap and my wine in hand, I settled in to start figuring out who I could beg for money, knowing it would be a while before I hit the shower and then climbed into bed.

As soon as I got comfortable, my doorbell rang.

Shit.

I definitely wasn't expecting company, and anybody who knew me *knew* better than to show up at my door unannounced. Unless, of course, there was some emergency. And based on the fact that it was already ringing again – impatiently so – I suspected that was the case.

Pulling myself up, I moved my laptop and wine to the coffee table and headed for the door as the ringing bell switched to a firm, LVPD-style knock. That made me pause for a second, but then I continued on, pressing up on my toes to look through my peephole when I reached the door.

I frowned.

Who the hell is she?

I took a step back, trying to place the vaguely-familiar face of the woman on the other side of my door. Before I could

10

though, that booming knock sounded again, so official that I worried something had happened with one of the kids.

That made me open the door.

"Can I help you?" I asked, peering through the few inches of space that the chain-latch allowed, once I'd unlocked and pulled the door open. The woman's lips – painted a perfect peachy-nude brown, even at nearly ten at night – curved into a smirk.

"No. But I can help *you*. Let's have a conversation."

My eyebrows pulled together, confused. "I… excuse me? Are you sure you have the right apartment?"

"Are you Rowan Phillips, age thirty-two, Program Director for the *Cartwright Center*?" she asked, her perfectly blown-out bob swaying a little as she tipped her head to the side, waiting for me to answer.

"Uh… yeah. Who are you?"

"Desiree Byers. Unhook the latch, Rowan. You and I need to talk."

I stood there looking stupid – or at least it felt that way – wondering what the hell a woman who looked, quite literally, like money, had to talk to me about. But it was that – the fact that she looked like money, which I needed – that made me do as she said.

I unlatched the door.

And immediately regretted it.

Before I could blink, there were people in my apartment – the two women in suits from before, barging past me to look in my bedroom, bathroom, and closets, and a man, in jeans and a hoodie, holding some device that he held up in the air as he walked through my space.

"Hey, what the hell is going on?!" I asked, making the mistake of stepping into the hoodie-wearer's face. Instantly, one

11

of the suits was on me, pulling my wrists behind my back to detain me, paying no mind to my demands to be let go until "Desiree" spoke up.

"Briana. Frankie. You're dismissed," she said, in a completely bored tone.

I didn't know who was who, but I was let go, and they disappeared while I was still rubbing my tender wrists.

"Eliot, are we good?" she asked one of her minions who remained, the one in the hoodie. He nodded, but then I watched, outraged, as he picked up my laptop and phone, taking them with him as he headed out the door.

"Excuse me, what the *fuck* is this?!" I asked, trying uselessly to follow him – but Briana or Frankie stepped into the doorway, blocking me.

"Rowan, please," Desiree said, in that same, overly-composed voice. "Your things will be returned to you as soon as we've talked. For now, come and sit down."

"Like hell!" I shot back. "I'll calmly come and sit when you tell me what you're doing here."

She smiled, then walked over to my threadbare sofa and gracefully draped her designer-suit clad body into a seat, clasping perfectly-manicured hands in her lap. "I plan to explain everything. When you come and sit down."

Frustrated, I pushed out a breath, shooting a last dirty look at Frankie or Briana or whoever before I stomped over to the couch. The door was closed, and Desiree reached for my remote, pausing the TV before she turned it off, then waited.

I ran my tongue over my lips as I sat down, fists clenched, ready to swing on *Desiree Byers* if necessary.

"Thank you Rowan," she said warmly, as if we were old friends, making it harder to shake the feeling that I knew who this woman was. "Let's get to business, shall we?"

12

"How do I know you?" I asked, not caring if it came across as rude. "*Do* I know you?"

She smiled. "You've probably heard of me. I have a working relationship with a lot of very important people in this city."

As soon as she said that, it clicked. "You're… that fixer, or whatever?"

"Uh, this isn't *Scandal*. I don't call myself that."

"Then what do you call yourself?"

"Desiree Byers. Nice to meet you, Rowan."

I huffed. "I cannot say the same."

"I think my proposal will change your mind," Desiree said, with another of those arrogant smirks that made me want to slap something. Not *her*, just… something.

"Proposal?"

She nodded. "Yes." Her hands went to a luxury bag that was probably worth more than everything I owned, combined, placing it on top of a coffee table that had seen better days. From it, she pulled a thick manila envelope, which she placed beside my wine bottle.

"The *Cartwright Center* needs money. My client has money. If you're willing, I believe that the two of you can come together for a mutually beneficial arrangement."

My eyes narrowed, top lip curled. "You *can't* be serious. Is this why you don't have a title, can't think of a prettier name for a *pimp*?"

"I am *not* a pimp," she shot back, with more bite than I expected. "Let's make that *very* clear. I am *only* here as a favor to a client who is special to me – this is absolutely not an item on my usual list of services."

"Who is the client?"

Desiree shook her head. "That is information that will remain undisclosed – he wishes to remain anonymous for the duration of the agreement."

"Oh *hell* no," I exclaimed, my head rearing back. "You think I'm crazy? I'm supposed to accept money to get chopped up and eaten by your stranger danger ass "special" client? That's what you think is about to happen?"

"Well he certainly has no plans to chop you up," Desiree laughed, like there was actually something funny here. "*Eating* you, however, is probably among his intentions, assuming of course that your full medical exam doesn't raise any red flags."

"Full medic—okay, you gotta go," I said, standing up. "And you can tell whatever creepy ass old white man sent you here that I'm not on the black girl fetish menu, okay?"

She laughed again, and didn't move. "Rowan, my client is neither old, nor white, and I wish that you would take a seat, and really give this some thought. You lost a huge grant today – a grant you deserved by the way, we looked at your application – and that center is on its last legs unless something big happens. Right?"

My nostrils flared as I shrugged. "And?"

"Hi," she said, with a little wave. "You can call me *something big.*"

"I'm not a prostitute."

Desiree raised an eyebrow. "No one said you were."

"And yet here you are, on my couch, offering me money to have sex with some weirdo stranger who can't get pussy for himself. It's *Vegas.* Why can't he just hire an escort like all the other rich men?"

"Because his situation is a bit more… delicate. He requires a certain level of discretion concerning his private life."

14

I snorted. "Who the hell is this guy? The president, the Black Panther, what? And I'm supposed to what… wear a blindfold while he screws me, then leaves an envelope of cash on the dresser? And again – *why me?* There are women who do this… as a profession. *Why me?*"

"Because you're the woman he chose. It's as simple as that. He's not the president, *or* the damn Black Panther, no, but he is a man of a certain standing in this city, that—"

"I will *not* help him cheat on his wife," I hissed, only for my words to be met with a shake of her head.

"You certainly won't, because he doesn't have one of those. Yes, you would be required to have your eyes covered at all times, but there would certainly be no envelope on the dresser. His offer is to cover any and all personal debt you have, as well as any debt for the center – including the cost of your desperately needed remodeling. Further, you would receive a lump sum – based on *your* calculations – large enough to cover utilities and any other reoccurring bills at the center for a year. That money would go into a trust, with you receiving a monthly stipend. Also in that trust would be the money necessary to fund your summer nutrition program, as well as daily meals of your choosing for roughly a hundred kids. In addition to that, my client would use his connections to solidify ongoing funding to keep the *Cartwright Center* open and serving this community for years to come. See? Way too much to fit in an envelope."

"Get. The. Hell. Out. Of. My. Apartment." I spat, storming toward the door to fling it open. "I don't know what the hell kind of game this is, or who sent you, but this shit isn't funny to me, and it stops *now. Go!*"

"I can assure you this isn't a ga—"

"*Go!*" I screamed, not caring about Frankie or whoever was standing there glaring in the open door.

Eyebrows raised, Desiree rose from her seat just as gracefully as she'd sat down. The manila envelope went back into her bag, and she strode confidently past me on sky-high pumps, stopping just on the other side of the door.

"Rowan… don't be foolish," she insisted, as my phone and laptop were passed back to me. "You're a bright young woman, and obviously passionate about your work with the children you serve at the center. This is an excellent opportunity, and I would hate to see you pass it up."

I stepped right into her face, and she didn't flinch, just stared, waiting for a response.

"*You* screw him then," I told her, earning myself one last smirk before I shut the door in her face.

And then immediately freaked out.

What the hell was that?

Was that for real?

*Was **she** for real?*

Would he really give me all that money for the center?

Those questions ran through my head at hyper-speed, melding together in a big, confused pile. Legal or not, having sex for money was something I'd never even considered, but honestly speaking… these stakes were a little different.

A *lot* different.

This wasn't… giving a stranger a blowjob behind a filthy dumpster for a twenty. This wasn't even… a high-end call girl, getting paid by the hour. This was… changed lives. Too many for me to count. This was… something I could never say yes to.

But I shouldn't say "no" without at least… thinking about it.

I snatched my front door open, hoping that I'd catch Desiree in the hall, waiting for the elevator. Instead, I found her right where I'd left her, eyebrow raised, with that cocky smirk still on her face as she held up that envelope.

Before I could say anything, she held it out to me, putting it in my hands.

"All the necessary details are here. You have twenty-four hours to think about it."

One of her minions reached for the door handle, pulling it closed, leaving me alone with the contract, a head full of questions, and twenty-four hours to decide if I was willing to sell myself for the good of the *Cartwright Center*.

- & -

"Did she say yes?" I asked, not bothering with a proper greeting once I saw it was Des' number that had lit my screen in the back of the darkened limo.

I wasn't surprised when Des laughed. "Come on, Mr. President. What do you think she said?"

"Stop calling me that, please," I grunted, shifting positions to drop my head back against the seat. "You know I hate that shit."

"Don't be such a stick in the mud, Reid," she teased. "Consider it a compliment."

"I consider it pressure – more pressure than I need right now, all things considered."

Des sighed. "Ah, pressure. That's what you need Ms. Phillips around to relieve, no?"

"Des…"

"*Fine*," she said, clearing her throat. "Ms. Phillips reacted like most women who've never considered a career in sex work would react – unfavorably. She was offended, like I expected."

"But?"

"*But...* she's desperate. Like I expected. She took the contract to look over. I gave her twenty-four hours. She'll call at nine or so tomorrow night to say yes, after she's reviewed the terms."

I closed my eyes. "How can you be so sure?"

"Because I am," she said, simply, and I believed her, because Des got shit done. She *always* got shit done. "I'll go ahead and schedule the medical exams and all that jazz, and put together the paperwork she'll want too. A week from now, you'll have your private plaything, and still be the man your constituents elected in public. Rest easy tonight, my friend."

"Thank you, Des."

"You're welcome."

With my eyes still closed, I dropped the phone into my lap, letting the image of Rowan Phillips come to the forefront of my mind. I'd never seen her before today, but that was all it took to know she was someone I'd never forget.

She wasn't... *polished.* For some reason, that stood out. She was pretty as hell – something that could've scored points in the shallow world of local politics she'd dipped her toe in by applying for that grant. But she hadn't played it up. Her smooth, red-brown skin appeared makeup-free, thick hair pulled into a simple ponytail, curves hidden underneath ill-fitting pants and a tee shirt with the name of her organization across the front. Her only adornment had been simple hoop earrings, but still, she'd stood out. Something about the determination, then hope, then disappointment in those expressive brown eyes... I wanted her.

18

But for me, it wasn't as simple as walking up and introducing myself - that was where Des came in.

I just hoped she was right, that Rowan would accept my offer, and get this ball rolling.

As far as I was concerned… waiting a whole week to have her was already too long.

Two.

"So we're doing this, right?"

I stopped mid-chew to raise an eyebrow at Laurel, my best friend in the world. She'd shown up – unannounced – at my door, too early in the morning for company, but she'd come bearing bagels, so my forgiveness was quick.

"I'm sorry – *we?*" I asked, once I'd swallowed my mouthful of food to turn from my closet to where she was perched on my bed, reading the contract that'd had me up all night.

She huffed, pulling a handful of braids over her shoulder. "Yes, *we*. I'm going to live through you as you tell me *every little detail* of what this man does to you. *Every detail.*"

"Lo, I need you thinking with logic, not libido!" I fussed, pulling a pair of jeans from the shelf. "I don't trust myself with this anymore, because the longer I think about it, the more I'm thinking about… maybe…actually… *doing* this. You have to talk me out of it."

Laurel cringed. "Yeah, uh… about that… I'm not going to do that. Because it's actually a great deal."

"That requires me to have sex with him, for a whole month!"

Slapping the papers down into her lap, Laurel shrugged. "And? I can count at least three fuckboys off the top of my head that you've given the pussy *for free*, for much longer than a month, so what exactly is your point?"

"I… I… this is… *this is different!*" I insisted.

"How?"

"It just *is*."

Rolling her eyes, Laurel stood, approaching me with her arms crossed as I switched the yoga pants I'd slept in for jeans. "You know what? You're right. It *is* different. It's *better*."

"Better?"

She nodded. "Yep. No games, no lies, no bullshit. You each know exactly what you're getting from this. Everything right up front."

"Yeah, everything except his name, or his face."

"Neither of which is relevant, to be honest. You aren't trying to fall in love – you're trying to get *paid*, so you can keep helping those bad ass kids."

"Kids are—"

"Not bad, yeah yeah, whatever you say," Laurel said, waving me off. "The point is, his name doesn't matter, and neither does his face – you'll never see it anyway. Who cares what he looks like – you're getting paid to cum. Why are you complaining?"

I shook my head. "No, see that's the thing – who says orgasms are on the menu for *me*? More likely – I'll just be laying there pretending to enjoy it, waiting for the shit to be over."

"Which brings me *back* to those fuckboys that you're so drawn to. At least with this, you'll be well-compensated for your troubles."

"I thought you were talking me *out* of this?" I asked, pulling a long-sleeved *Cartwright Center* tee on over my bra. "I shared this because I need help."

"Bullshit. You already know what you should do – already know what you're *going* to do. We both know you aren't walking away from an opportunity like this. You would do *anything* for that place, because of what it did for you. So I think it's time for this conversation to shift away from *if* you're going to do this, to how to do it safely. I'm calling my big sister."

"You are *not*," I hissed, dropping the pair of socks I'd just pulled from my drawer to snatch the cell phone from Laurel's hands. "I do not need anybody else knowing about this, Lo!"

"Give me back my phone!" she yelled, practically crawling over my back as I turned away. "You know Willow is legit – she's not going to tell anybody!"

"It's not about that!" I shoved Laurel away, and tucked her phone into my bra before I propped my hands on my hips. "It's one thing for *you* to know – you know all my dirty little secrets, and I know all of yours. But *this?*"

Laurel sucked her teeth, and then walked up to me and shamelessly reached into my cleavage for her phone. "Girl, *goodbye.* Willow met the dude she's screwing now at an anonymous sex club, with masks and shit. *She* is not going to judge you."

"She wasn't *paid.*"

"Sounds like *her* bad to me," Laurel countered, tapping something into her phone. "But… if you want to keep it in on the low, I totally understand, and I'm gonna respect that. I won't tell her the details, I'll just have her get me some equipment we can use – tracking device to make sure we know where you are, maybe… a safe word or something, that if you say it, it automatically triggers your phone to call the police. I actually know someone who is working on an app like that, maybe I'll reach out…"

I blew out a sigh. "*Shit.*"

"What is it?"

I shook my head. "As soon as you said "police", this whole scenario played out in my mind. I scream "gorgonzola" because this crazy motherfucker is killing me, so my phone calls the police, and who shows up?"

Laurel grinned. "Cree."

"Yeah. Bingo."

"I would die *for* you," Laurel laughed, as I shook my head.

My relationship with Cree was… hard to describe. The easiest thing to call him would be an ex – one of the fuckboys Laurel had thought of earlier – but he was more than that. He was a confidant, a friend, a protector with the authority of a badge. I'd known him since I was twelve years old, and had been moved into the same foster home as him. It wasn't until we'd both aged out of the system that we were ever romantic, and our "love affair" was messy and short-lived. Somehow, that hadn't ruined our comradery, and I now thought of him as what he should have remained in the first place – a kind of big brother.

"Can you *imagine* explaining the whole thing to him? I'd be so embarrassed!"

"Girl Cree would kill his ass," Laurel giggled. "I still don't understand how you managed to go from backshots to protective big brother with him, but I need you to teach me your ways."

I shook my head as I sat down at the end of the bed to put my socks on. "I have no *ways*, ma'am. I have no swagger. Nobody worth a damn is checking for me."

"You realize those words mean nothing to me when there is a literal contract for your pussy right here on the bed? Buddy is coming out of major dollars for you. I demand you tell me where you met a man this rich, and explain how to get an offer of my own. My closet app isn't going to build itself – I could use a sponsor too."

Sitting up straight, I planted my hands on either side of me on the bed. "Girl, if I knew, you'd be the first person I told. I've been wracking my brain trying to figure out *why me*. I mean… he had to have met me or something, right?"

"Yeah… he has to have at least seen you. And didn't you say this Desiree chick claimed they'd read your grant proposal? So he has to be somebody with money and clout, right?"

I nodded. "Right. You know… I wonder if we could find a list of her clients or something, and figure this out?"

"No chance," Laurel said, frowning. "There's no way she has a *list* – public or private. And if the client requires this level of anonymity… I doubt he would even be seen with Desiree Byers in public. She only shows her face with clients on some power trip shit. I still can't believe you met her. Is she as bad in person as she is on the internet?"

"Absolutely. Like Olivia Pope in the flesh. Hell, badder."

"Damn."

"Exactly." I pushed out a sigh and then stood, going to the vanity mirror over my dresser. I frowned a little as I took in my bare face, standard ponytail, and plain ass clothes – my everyday look for my work at the center. "*Why me?*" I muttered to myself, temporarily forgetting that Laurel was in the room.

I was quickly reminded though, as she rushed up beside me. "Uh, because you're gorgeous, Ro. *That's* why."

"No," I shook my head. "Like, I'm not downing myself or anything. I don't think I'm unattractive, I'm just… regular. A guy with money like this… in a city like this… I don't know. I would think he'd choose a woman who… gets her hair done, and dresses well, and takes the time to throw on a little eyeliner, at least. The Desirees of the world, you know?"

Laurel shrugged. "Eh. I guess I get your point, but hell… maybe the fact that you're *not* is exactly why he wants you. But um…before you go see him, you're getting your damn hair done, and putting a face on, right?"

"Obviously," I scoffed. "I just…*God*, I don't know about this. This is nuts. I have to get a physical to do this. I have to sign

24

a non-disclosure agreement if I do this. I have to agree not to even go on a date for the whole month of the agreement."

I walked away, stepping into my closet for my shoes, but I could feel Laurel rolling her eyes behind me.

"Girl, you know damn well you weren't going on a date anyway," she teased. "And the contract stipulates that your only sexual contact will be with each other for the month. So, he's obligated to monogamy too."

I sucked my teeth as I grabbed my tennis shoes. "Because a legal obligation *ever* stopped a man from pulling his dick out. Right."

"I'm just saying," Laurel laughed. "You're acting like this is a bad deal, but the way the contract reads, it sounds like it's designed so that you'll be happy too. It doesn't seem one-sided."

"I *know*," I told her, as I walked back to the bed. "I just… I can't believe I'm really considering this. Am I really considering this?"

Laurel smirked. "Rewind back to where I explained that it wasn't even really in question. You're doing this. I know it. You know it. Desiree Byers knows it. It's really just a matter of when you're going to call her."

I pushed out a deep sigh as I pulled on my sneakers. They seemed even more worn than usual today – frayed laces, stitching that was well past prime, scuffed toes. This was the point I'd reached now – so devoted to the *Cartwright Center* that I couldn't even afford to replace my damn shoes.

Swallowing the lump in my throat, I pulled them on, determined not to give old feelings of inferiority any space in my head. They were useless, especially when I knew I wasn't defined by what was on my feet.

Still though… speaking practically…this was no way to live.

Not when I, finally, had the option to change it.

And make a real difference.

"Tonight. I'm calling her tonight."

"Come on, Kev! Let's see a little more hustle!" I yelled, clapping as the kid in question ran toward me from third base. My words prompted him to move a *little* faster, but the afternoon sun was a coach's worst nightmare on a sunny day like today. It was talking *way* louder than I was.

Still, even if they were only giving half-efforts at practice in the energy-draining heat, I felt good that I'd gotten them outside at all, doing something to get their little hearts and legs pumping.

I looked up as a whistle – not mine – sounded, and found Mila and another volunteer, Cody, heading in our direction wearing big smiles. A smile grew on my face too as I took note of the bright red cooler they carried between them, hoping they were about to make my day.

Especially since they were interrupting practice.

"What is this?" I asked, as soon as they were in earshot. "That cooler isn't one of ours."

"Bottled water," Mila gushed. "I have to take the cooler back to the school when we're done, but I rescued all these from food services. The school switched vendors, so they can't stock this brand anymore or something. Can you believe they were going to just throw them away?" she asked, flipping the lid open to start handing them out to the hot, thirsty kids.

My eyes got big. "At your university?" I asked, and she nodded. "Wow. *Great* save. Kids, remember to put those bottles in the recycle bin please!" I yelled, as they started running off. I got a small chorus of *"yes ma'ams"* before they'd all gotten as far away as they could from practice, opting for the shade closer to the building.

"So, I've been thinking," Mila said, flipping the lid of the cooler closed. "We should reach out to some local business owners, about donations."

I raised an eyebrow. "Yeah, me too. We've been doing that. Everybody in a five-block radius has heard my begging."

She shook her head. "No, not just in the neighborhood, like... the city. Like... the strip. The casinos, the hotels—"

"Oh absolutely *not*," I told her, shaking my head. "I've never met one that didn't want their face or name plastered all over the building for a minor donation. Or worse – wanted to turn the *Cartwright Center* into an ad for their debauchery. No thanks."

Mila pushed out a sigh as her shoulders dropped. "Damn. I really thought I was onto something that could make a difference."

Shit.

"Well, let me walk that back a bit." I grabbed her hand, and squeezed. "If *you* want to reach out, I say go for it. It's been a few years, so maybe they've evolved – it never hurts to ask. But remember – maintaining the integrity of this center is paramount. A check won't change that."

She nodded. "Yes, of course! We don't want to get money from just anywhere, right?"

I cleared my throat. "Well... uh... it's more about the intention behind the money, than the source. Any donation we accept can't have conditions we aren't willing to meet. The donor can't think that their check means they own us, or that they have some sort of say. *We* are the backbone of this place."

"Understood," Mila told me with a smile. I could already see her wheels turning to figure out her pitch to the potential donors. "I think I'm going to set up in-person meetings if I can. Or – *oooh*, catch them out and about or something. Conveniently in a lowcut top," she said, leaning in to speak in a low voice. "God didn't give me titties this nice for no reason, right? Boobs for charity!"

She laughed at what she clearly intended as a joke, and I did too, even though I felt a little sick about it. Mila was young, incredibly bright, and incredibly beautiful – and obviously not oblivious to the fact that she could use all three of those factors as currency in our society. Still… I didn't want that for her.

"While I appreciate your enthusiasm, our cause can speak for itself – no boobs needed," I gently scolded, making sure to temper it with a laugh. Thankfully, Mila's bubbly nature shined through, preserving the light moment.

"Alright, I'll try it your way first, but I'm telling you now – if I see another *final notice* on one of those bills, I'm walking up to one of those Drake hotel twins with *my* twins out. Somebody is gonna write this place a dang check," she laughed, offering me a wave as she headed off with the cooler, to pass out water to a fresh wave of kids coming for the after-school services.

I was a hypocrite.

There was no way of getting around it.

I didn't want Mila using her looks to garner donations for this place, didn't want her to have to fall back on such tactics… while Desiree Byers' business card was practically burning a hole in my pocket.

I'd been thinking about it all day, and my decision was made, for the most part. I didn't want to see another *final notice*

28

bill either, and agreeing to this completely ridiculous arrangement seemed like my only viable, long-term option.

"Ms. Ro! Ms. Ro!"

I snapped out of my depressing thoughts long enough to see a pack of preschool-aged girls headed in my direction, already giggling. There was nothing I could do to help the smile they brought to my face as they swarmed me, holding on to my legs.

"*Fweeze Pops!*" they demanded, and I laughed, nodding.

Of course, it was that time of day. Like clockwork, they came to me requesting the frozen treats as a reprieve from... whatever they'd faced that day, happy times or not. If I couldn't do anything else to be a bright spot, I could do *that.*

As long as we're here.

"Come on babies," I sang, laughing as they quickly made a line behind me, following me straight to the kitchen inside. I stopped in front of the deep freezer, turning to them with a little smile as I stalled on doling the treats out. "What is the *magic* word, hmmm?"

"Pweeeze Ms. Ro?!"

My little smile grew into a big grin as I nodded. "Yes my sweethearts, you know it!" I flipped up the lid to the freezer with a flourish and reached inside to where we kept the freezer pops, but froze when my hand connected with warm plastic.

"*No,*" I whispered, tears instantly forming behind my eyelids as I took in the scene in front of me. The bottom of the freezer was a soupy mess of melted ice cream sandwiches, the treats the kids had asked for were back to their liquid state, and hundreds and hundreds of dollars of hot dogs and hamburgers – food Cody was supposed to put on the grill and sell at the upcoming softball game – was slowly rotting in the warm freezer.

"Ms. *Roooo* freeze popssss!" a little voice demanded, and I dropped the lid of the freezer and covered my face with my hands, shaking my head.

"I… I can't right now baby I'm sorry," I said, trying to keep it together.

"Rowan… what's wrong?"

I peeked through my fingers to see Mila at the doorway to the kitchen, frowning. "The freezer…" Instead of saying more, I simply shook my head, and from the look on her face, she caught on.

"No fweeze pops?" another kid asked, her hurt feelings apparent in her voice – a sound that instantly made the lump in my throat even bigger.

"You know what?" I asked, attempting to sound cheerful as I hurried past them, to my office. "I have an idea!" I pulled out my keys and unlocked my desk, retrieving my wallet. My hands shook as I pulled out my one, lonely credit card. My "emergency" card, with a tiny credit limit and absurd interest rate. I used my free hand to wipe away a stray tear, and then turned to hand the card to Mila.

"Go flag down an ice cream truck or something. Or… run to the store, and get these babies some popsicles. It's *not* a day at the Cartwright Center if we can't even have popsicles, right?" I asked the kids who'd followed Mila and me to the office.

Of course, they were excited about the prospect, but Mila looked unconvinced, glancing between me and that credit card with a frown. "Rowan… are you sure?"

"Yes," I snapped, without intending to. "I… I'm sorry, I didn't mean to—"

"I get it, Ro. You're good."

I nodded, then turned away from her, focusing my attention out the window. "Okay. So… you go work out some popsicles, and I… am going to call somebody about this freezer. And about the food.”

"But we can't af—"

"Popsicles, Mila. Please?"

She pushed out a sigh, but she nodded. "Popsicles. Yeah."

As soon as she left, kids in tow, I closed the door behind her, pressing my back to it after I'd flipped the lock. I didn't even fight it as my knees buckled and I sank to the ground, face in my hands as I broke into sobs.

I let myself have a few minutes of that, but then I shook my head, knowing what I needed to do. I fished Desiree's card from my pocket, and grabbed my cell phone, dialing the number on the front. She answered on the third ring, confident and competent while I sat on peeling, ancient linoleum feeling useless.

"Ms. Phillips, I hope this call means that you've decided to accept my client's offer."

I swallowed hard. "Uh… yeah. I mean, yes. Yes, it does."

"Excellent! Let me know your availability for tomorrow, and we'll get you in for your physical. If all is well, we'll sign paperwork and move forward. You can have a check in your hand in as little as 48 hours," she chirped.

"Yeah. About that," I said, swallowing yet again, trying to bring moisture to my dry throat. "I need a favor. *Tonight.*"

There was silence on the line for several long seconds, and then…

"I'm listening. Go on."

Yes.

Yes.

She said yes.

Des' words echoed in my head, making something like relief sink into my shoulders.

"Reid, are you still there? You didn't pass out from happiness, did you?"

I chuckled at her teasing as I shook my head. "No, not quite. So what's next?"

"Well, she's getting her medical exam tomorrow, and then we do paperwork, and then... she's all yours."

"Perfect."

"There was something else though," Des added, knowing I was preparing to end the call. "She... asked for a favor."

My excitement waned. "She did?"

"Oh yes she most certainly did, and I just want you to know that I feel a way about it."

I dipped my head, eyes closed as I pressed the phone closer to my ear. "What did she want?"

Des huffed. "*Well*, do you know that woman had the absolute *gall* to ask me if I could help her... get a new freezer for the center, and fill it with the kind of cheap, processed meats that go best on buns. The one she had went out."

Immediately, I laughed. "You're serious?"

"I'm serious. All the eligible women in this sinful city, and you ask Mary friggin' Poppins for a sex contract. Only you, Reid."

My lips spread into a grin. "So you took care of it, right? Used the account I set up?"

"No. I mean, yes, I took care of it. No, I didn't use your account. This one is on me. Ms. Phillips managed to tug my heartstrings."

"I didn't know you had those, Des," I teased.

32

She laughed. "Yeah, well now you do. I will update you tomorrow, after the medical exam."

"Thank you."

"You're welcome."

I hung up with Des and put my phone down on the table, reaching for my fork with a renewed appetite after hearing such good news.

"I'm glad to see a smile on your face, my love, but many people would find answering the phone at the dinner table quite rude."

There goes my appetite again.

My fork dropped from my fingers, clattering on the table as I clasped my hands. My elbows dug into the hardwood surface as I propped my chin on my fists, and glared across the table at my fiancée.

"Well, *my love*," I started, not bothering to filter my sarcastic tone. "Many people would find the fact that you let another man stick his dick down your throat *quite rude*, but what do I know about proper etiquette, huh?"

Instantly, the smug grin dropped from Enid's face, replaced by a scowl. "Obviously not much. How *dare* you speak to me that way?"

"Oh baby… if you think that was rough, you'd *really* be scandalized by what I haven't said."

She sat back in her seat, pushing her freshly-done weave away from her face. "How many times have I said I was sorry?"

"How many times have I said I don't give a fuck? Not that I believe you anyway."

"*Why not?*" she hissed – a question that brought back my smile.

"Why *not?*" I repeated. "Why *would* I? You were laid up with another motherfucker with my mother's heirloom ring on

33

your hand, and I have the pictures to prove it because your ass was too stupid to exercise some fucking tact. Or maybe because of the abortion you don't know that *I* know you had, without speaking a single word to me about being pregnant – *probably* because you couldn't be sure who the father was. Does that answer your question?"

For a second, she was silent. Eyes wide, mouth open, struck by the revelation I'd just made. Then, she suddenly stood, so fast that her chair went flying backward, hitting the floor with a loud thump.

"I do *not* have to take this from you Reid. I'm *done*," she screamed, snatching off her ring and launching it toward my chest.

I caught it, and was out of my chair and on her in seconds, stopping her before she pushed her way through the dining room door.

"See that's where you're dead ass wrong," I growled, right in her face. "You're *not* done. You *will* take it. Because you have as much riding on this as I do, and you know it."

"Then I guess you'd better be a little nicer, hmm?" she asked – or rather, purred, grinning as she pushed her body against mine.

I shook my head, realizing that my anger was exactly the reaction she'd wanted.

"Nah. Don't count on it," I told her, pushing the ring into my pocket. "Thank you for finally taking that off. I've been trying to figure out how to get it without breaking your fingers. We'll get you something else to wear. And you *will* wear it. You *will* act like you have some fucking sense. You *will* use some damn discretion while you're running around with your little boyfriend."

34

She pouted. "What boyfriend? I messed up, fine. But that's over. There's only *you*, my love."

"Don't insult me," I whispered into her hair, then planted a kiss on her forehead. "We both know the truth."

Her hands went to my belt buckle, and tugged. "Let me make it up to you. Right here. Right now. You haven't touched me in months, Reid... I know you're *starving*."

"You're right," I told her, grabbing her hands. "I am." I lifted one of my hands to her chin, cupping it to stare into her beautiful, campaign-perfect face. "But every time I look at you... I lose my appetite."

I dropped her chin and stepped away, not bothering to go back to my plate. I grabbed my phone and headed out, leaving my fiancée standing in the dining room alone.

I had plans to make.

Three

It was almost perfect.

A day at the center – the day before the big softball game, actually. The brand-new fridge and freezer were filled to the brim with food, and the kids were taking full advantage. And we were *letting* them.

"Eat as much as you want, sweetheart."

Being able to say those words filled me with the kind of joy I couldn't even describe, and it made the kids happy, which made the volunteers happy. Everybody was happy.

Except… there was still the little matter of what I'd had to do in order to make this happen.

What I *still* had to do.

I was trying not to think about it, because thinking about it made it even more real, which I didn't need. For the moment, I could just look at it as a distant, vague responsibility, and focus on living in this moment of good energy.

Well… I could until Desiree walked into the building.

She was obviously out of place among the timeworn surroundings of the center, with her designer wardrobe, perfect hair, and badass female bodyguards. Still, she wore a smile on her face as she sauntered up to me, waving at the kids. Cool and collected, while I was about to have a heart attack.

"Ms. Byers!" I said, rushing up to her before one of the volunteers could ask a question. "How can I help you?"

"I was just coming to make sure the new appliances had been installed, and that you were happy with the delivery. But," she glanced around the little cafeteria. "It looks like everything is on the up and up."

I nodded. "Yes, it is. And thank you again."

"Oh, you don't have to thank me. But, you do have to come with me. Your presence has been requested for the night, and since this is the uh... first time... I thought I'd procure you myself instead of sending one of my companions in for you."

My eyebrow went up. "Excuse me? Procure me?"

"Yes, Ms. Phillips. You do remember the terms of the arrangement, don't you? He calls, you... come." She smirked after she said that, obviously pleased with her little joke.

I wasn't amused.

I glanced up to see that Mila had entered the dining room, and was standing with the other volunteers. Whispering, watching, and undoubtedly wondering why in the world I was talking to a woman like this.

Grabbing Desiree at the elbow, I pulled her a little closer to the door, out of view – and earshot – of anyone else. "Are you serious with this? He wants me now? I have a softball game tomorrow, and—"

"*Not* that it's relevant, but you'll make it to your game, Rowan. Right now though, you will let your volunteers know that you need them to take over, because you have something to *do*. My client's schedule is tight, and part of the agreement is that you *will* work around it. Starting now. Meet me at the car in two minutes."

With that, she turned and walked off, leaving no room for argument. And because I didn't doubt that she meant what she said, I didn't waste time getting back into the dining room to pull Mila aside.

"What the *hell* is Desiree Byers doing here?" she gushed, as soon as we were in semi-private. "Was it her? It was her, wasn't it? The angel donor, that gave the appliances? How do you know her?!"

"I…" I shook my head, then pushed out a sigh. "I'll have to explain later. Right now though, I have to go with her. Can you close up for me?"

"Of course. Why are you going with her? Can I come too? Are you meeting more donors?"

"It's complicated," I told her, holding up my hands to get her to stop. "But listen… thank you, okay?"

"Yeah, no problem. Go. *Go*," she insisted, pushing me toward the door.

Knowing I was running on a tight limit, I didn't prolong it. I grabbed my things from my office and headed out, climbing into the back of the sleek black SUV that was waiting out front.

As it pulled off, I looked to Desiree, whose attention was buried in her phone. For the first few minutes, I was fine, but the longer we drove, the more my stomach knotted, the rawer my nerves became, until I was feeling anxious, and… agitated.

"Are you proud of yourself?" I asked, out of nowhere, and immediately wished I could take back. But since I couldn't – and since Desiree was looking at me know, undoubtedly wondering if I'd lost my mind – I had to press on. "For this. Bullying poor, desperate women into selling themselves? Is this where you thought you'd be when you got your law degree? Part of the sex trade?"

Desiree's eyebrows went way up, and she turned off her phone, giving me her full attention, with a look that would've killed me, no question, if she had such superpowers.

"You are *no* victim," she said slowly, deliberately. "You were presented an offer, you took it, now you sit there and wait while you're driven to a luxury hotel, to put on designer lingerie, and fuck a man you don't even have to look at for the nice big check and other perks you *agreed* to receive. If you want to back out now? *Fine.* We can stop this car, you can keep the freezer and the food, and my client will write you a ten thousand dollar check for your consideration. Or you can do what you agreed to. The choice is yours. But that's just it – a *choice.* Do not dare sit across from me and accuse me of selling you into the sex trade. Don't play those games with *me.*"

I swallowed hard. "I didn't mean to—"

"Offend me, I know. But you did. And it's fine. You're ashamed of yourself. You're confused, and scared, I get it. But… you have a choice here, Rowan. If you decide to move forward, you should know… I would not send another woman – *especially* one I admire – into an unsafe situation with a man. No harm will come to you from him. Okay?"

"Yeah. Fine. Whatever," I responded, trying to save whatever little pride I could after getting lit into that way. sitting back in my seat, I crossed my arms as I sifted through my thoughts.

I'd messed up.

Not about the agreement in general - that was debatable anyway. But it definitely did me no good to antagonize Desiree, when hers was the only name or face I knew associated with this.

It was probably best to chill.

So that was exactly what I did, after I took the time to shoot a text to Laurel, letting her know what was going on. She'd hooked me up with some souped-up tracking app that she swore would get through any attempts to block it, and I believed her, knowing what she and her tech genius sister were capable of. If nothing else, I had that to help me feel better.

When I noticed a difference in surroundings through the windows I looked up, just in time to see the Drake Hotel signage before we pulled into a private parking garage, traveling several levels underground before the vehicle came to a stop.

As soon as it did, Desiree finally gave me her attention again. "Here's how this will work. You have roughly an hour to go to the room and get ready. Everything you need is there to shower, shave your legs, whatever. Take this time to do whatever you need to do get yourself together, and look your absolute best."

"You grabbed me from the center," I reminded her, confused. "I'm in jeans and a sweaty tee shirt, my hair is a mess, I'm tired, I—"

"Sounds to me like you've got work to do then. The lingerie my client requested is waiting for you upstairs... As well as a mini bar. If you need to pour yourself a shot or two to relax, do it."

I nodded, even though I still had a million questions in my mind. I was a pretty firm believer in experience being the best teacher, so at this point... It was time to just do it.

"So is this how it will always be? Somebody just picking me up at whatever time, no matter the inconvenience?"

Desiree shook her head. "No. After tonight, he'll let me know how often he wants to see you, and I'll work out a schedule. I'll try to let you know at least two days in advance, but there might be times that he wants to see you immediately, no matter what the schedule says. And you agreed to that."

I sighed. "Yeah. I did."

I reached for the door handle to get out, but Desiree stopped me, reminding me I didn't know where I was going.

"You'll need this," she said, pressing a key card into my hand, then closing my fingers around it. "When you get into the elevator, put the card in the slot. It'll automatically take you to the right floor. Once you're there, turn the card over, and use it to

40

open the door to the suite. Put your cell phone and purse in the tray beside the door. Once you're ready for the client, you pick up the phone in the bedroom, dial "313", and then put on the mask that's there."

"And then?"

"Then you wait. He'll come to you."

I swallowed another heavy breath, then gave Desiree a nod before I opened the door and climbed out, taking my purse with me. A huge part of me wanted to look back, wanted to ask Desiree to walk me up, so I wouldn't be alone.

But I wasn't a child.

I was a grown woman, who'd made a grown-ass decision, and now it was time for me to face the responsibility of what I'd signed up for.

Following the instructions Desiree had given, I made my way to a suite that took my breath away. Dark, polished stone floors, marble counters, big windows, lush fabrics – I'd seen stuff like this on TV, but had never seen surrounded by it in real life. I took a few minutes to look around, to touch the supple leather of the sofa, peek out the windows at the view, and simply take it all in before I made my way to the back.

To the bedroom.

Trying not to focus on the bed, I went straight to the bathroom, where I stripped down to climb into the extravagance of the shower. The shelf there was lined with everything high-end versions of everything I could possibly need, including shampoo and conditioner, so I cleaned myself from head to toe, figuring wet hair was better than sweaty hair.

In the cabinet under the vanity, I found a variety of products and perfumes, so I set to work pulling together a passable wash-n-go style for my hair, and making sure I smelled good. There was a makeup bag equipped with enough for a full

41

face, but with the limited time I had, I opted for simple liner and gloss.

When I stepped back into the bedroom, I took the time to really look around, and noticed flowers and a box on the dresser I hadn't paid attention to before. There was a card attached to the flowers, which I quickly ripped open, greedily scanning the words for anything that would bring some reality back to the unreal situation I'd put myself in.

"Looking forward to meeting you today. I hope the feeling is mutual."

Frustrated, I tossed the card down.

"Meeting" someone required a face to face interaction, being able to look them in their eyes. Being able to *see* them.

That's not what was happening.

Instead of dwelling on that, I pulled the box open. I had to dig through soft tissue paper to get to the contents, but once I got there, my mouth dropped open. I'd *never* touched lingerie that looked like that.

For the first time, a little tingle of excitement rushed through me, courtesy of the black-and-white bra, panties, and garter belt in that box. Goosebumps spread over my arms as I carefully put each piece on, even the stockings that attached to the garter belt, then moved to the mirror to look at myself.

I'd never found myself plagued by the belief that I wasn't an attractive woman. I considered myself such, and had been told so often. But, I rarely – if ever – had occasion to dress up, and had even less reason to put on sexy lingerie. After this though… maybe I'd make up some reasons.

I looked *amazing*.

Even with my "imperfect" body – stretch marks here and there, love handles, etc – the quality and construction of this

42

lingerie made it to where your eyes were too busy with my breasts and ass to be bothered with looking at anything else.

As I moved back and forth in the mirror, it struck me how, at that moment, I looked very little like "Ms. Ro", who handed out popsicles and books and helped with homework and coached softball. *That* was who I was. The woman in the mirror with the buttery-soft skin, big natural hair fluffed around her shoulders, dressed in lingerie she couldn't afford to purchase for herself, in a hotel room that probably cost more for one night than her monthly rent... she was someone else.

She - *I... needed* to be someone else.

That was the only way I was going to go through with this.

Maybe Rowan Phillips, with degrees in social work and childhood education couldn't sleep with a man in exchange for the list of benefits in that contract, but *Ro* could. It was corny, and I knew it, but if it got the job done, whatever.

My bolder, sexier, alter-ego put the lacy black mask over her head, dialed *313* on the phone by the bed, and then sat down, pulling the mask over her eyes to wait.

And wait.

And... *wait.*

But nothing happened.

After twenty minutes, I stood up, put on the silk robe that matched the lingerie, and went to that window to push my mask up and look out over the busy lights of the city.

Alter-ego my ass, I thought, shaking my head. It was a cool concept, sure, but if I were honest with myself... I was still terrified.

I shouldn't be here.

No sooner than the thought ran through my mind, the air in the room shifted as my ears picked up the sound of footsteps.

Swallowing hard, I fought the urge go sprinting toward the sound, mask up, satisfying my curiosity to see Desiree's "client".

But I suspected her guarantee of my safety went hand in hand with my adhesion to the rules that had been set. If I broke them, there was a good chance that what would have been an easy way to solve my financial troubles would turn into a nightmare. So I chose integrity, since I was already compromising my morality.

I pulled the mask down.

Moments later, those footsteps reached the bedroom, and stopped. At least, the sound did, muffled by the thick, plush surface of the carpet. I knew he was in the room because I could feel him there, but instead of saying anything, I turned back to the window, tightening the belt of my robe as I moved. I took a deep breath, willing myself not to start hyperventilating over what I had to do.

"Would I be correct in my observation if I told you that you seemed nervous?" he asked, and the deep, rich timbre of his voice sent an immediate tremble through me.

I clutched my arms around my waist, and nodded. "Yes. You would."

"Well… if it helps at all, I have no plans to score your performance. If that's what you're nervous about."

"I'm nervous because I've never done anything like this before."

"Neither have I," he claimed, from much closer than he'd been a moment ago. "And if my circumstances were different, I would have simply approached you the first time I saw you."

"Which was where?"

He laughed – a sound that warmed me from head to toe. "Now you know I can't tell you that, Ms. Phillips. That would help you figure out who I was, and we can't have that, can we?"

"You could just tell me. I signed ten different non-disclosures. I wouldn't say anything."

"Not a risk I can take, although for the record, I believe you."

He was right beside me now – probably facing the window just like I was. Only when he looked out, he saw lights, and cars, and the ant-sized people moving along the walkways many floors below us on The Strip.

All I saw was nothing.

"What would you like me to call you?" I asked, feeling indignant again. "Sir? Master? Your Highness?"

Again, he laughed. "No. I've been accused of arrogance, but I try to make a point of not being insufferable. You can call me Nick."

"Obviously not your actual name."

"It's a variation that I'm comfortable with. May I touch you?"

Behind my mask, my eyes narrowed, even though I couldn't see anything. His *requesting* to touch me struck me as odd, since I'd essentially signed myself over to him. He didn't have to ask for my permission, and yet... he did.

"Uh... yes. It's fine."

I held my breath a little, expecting him to immediately go for my ass underneath the robe. Instead, he turned me to face him, saying nothing as he pulled my crossed arms apart, then unbelted the robe.

And... there it was.

The beginning of my "belonging" to him.

A deeply appreciative sound left his throat as he pushed the robe from my shoulders, letting it drop to the floor around my feet. I couldn't see him, but I could certainly feel his gaze on me, lingering over my breasts, and then my ass, as he circled me.

45

"You look even better in this than I expected," he said, stopping in front of me. The fresh, woodsy scent of his cologne tickled my nose, making me breathe it in a little deeper, further consuming my senses. "I knew it would be perfect for you as soon as I saw it."

I swallowed. "Oh? You picked it yourself?" I asked, trying not to sound or look as nervous as I felt.

"Why wouldn't I? Do you not like it?"

"No," I answered immediately. "It's not that, at all. It's beautiful."

"*You* are beautiful."

I gasped as he suddenly grabbed me by the wrists, hauling me against him. There was definite strength in his grasp – this was no old, frail man. This was a broad chest, and good cologne, and a sexy voice, and definite arousal pressed against my stomach. Those things should have relieved me – instead, they raised my anxiety even further, to the point that I snatched away from him, taking several quick steps across the room.

"I *can't* do this," I insisted, reaching for the mask. I only got it pushed halfway over my eyes before "Nick" was on me, grabbing me from behind to clamp his big hands around my wrists.

"Rowan *stop*," he growled in my ear, making me whimper as his arms closed around me, wrapping me tight to keep me still. "You *know* you're supposed to keep the mask on at all times when I'm here."

I twisted my shoulders, trying in vain to get free. "I don't *care!*" I yelled, heart racing as he held me tighter.

"But I do," he told me, in a much calmer voice. "And you *should*. There is too much at stake, for too many people, for you to simply walk out of here after you've seen my face."

"Are you *threatening* me?"

46

"I am *warning* you," he corrected. "You can leave at any time you want to, if you don't want to be here. I don't get off on assault, Rowan. You can leave right now, and I promise you, you won't be bothered again. But if you *stay* – if you want those things I offered, the things for the center – you must follow the rules. And you have to decide. Right now."

I sucked in a shaky breath, trying to calm my heart before it shot right out of my chest. With the way the mask had slipped up, I could see just a sliver underneath – enough to see his hands clutching my arms, enough to see the smooth, deep brown of skin a few shades darker than mine.

"*Decide*," he growled, making me flinch a little as I shut my eyes tight. Of course I wanted to leave, and forget this had ever happened, settling right back into the safe bubble of my own little world. But there was another part of me – the part that signed the contract in the first place, the part that felt sexy as hell is this lingerie, and *horny* as hell in "Nick's" arms…that wanted to stay.

Needed to stay.

Needed to see this through.

Needed something that wasn't bills, or juvenile court, or alphabet charts.

"I'll stay."

I could practically feel his relief as his hold on me loosened, just enough that I could breathe a little easier. A moment later, his lips were on my skin, and I melted right into his touch. As if, less than a minute ago, I hadn't been ready to run away screaming.

My mouth opened for a whimper at the warm, wet sensation of his tongue on my neck, followed shortly by his teeth, for a gentle nip that paralyzed me for a moment. Long enough for him to let me go, pull my mask securely down over my eyes, and then pull me back into his arms.

I... hadn't been touched in a while.

Between the time I put in at the center, and my lack of patience for dealing with men, sex and romance had been off my radar. Now though, my mental sirens were blaring loud, in the form of hard nipples and wet panties and a strong desire to beg him to never stop doing what he was doing to my neck with his mouth.

A shudder rushed through me as his hands closed over my lace-covered breasts, cupping and squeezing. Briefly, I hoped he wasn't sucking my neck hard enough to leave a mark, but that thought was quickly overwhelmed by pleasure as he found my nipples, pinching them through the soft lace. My mouth fell open, panting as one of his hands slipped lower, past the garter belt and into my flimsy underwear.

Very, very quickly, his fingers pushed me damn near to the point of hyperventilation. When he slid further, sinking his middle and index fingers into me while the heel of his hand ground against my clit, I gave up on breathing altogether. My hand closed around his wrist, wanting and *not* wanting him to stop.

This felt... *different.*

Maybe it had been so long that I'd forgotten what stimulation at someone else's hand felt like. Or maybe it was the blindfold – the lack of sight heightening my other senses, making me more sensitive, more entuned. Either way, I was sliding towards an orgasm at record speed... until he stopped.

Confusion made me frown as he pulled away, but it quickly gave way to surprise as he turned me in his direction. His hands came to face, holding me where he wanted me for the next thing which, to my surprise, was a kiss.

48

And not just *any* kiss.

I whimpered into his mouth as his lips took over mine, gentle but insistent. After a moment, his tongue pressed the seam of my lips, seeking an invitation that I readily gave, opening myself to be devoured.

His hands went to my waist, pulling me into him as his tongue dipped into my mouth, caressing mine. I could feel his dick against my stomach again, heavy and hot and begging to be free, which I expected to happen at any moment.

But it didn't.

What happened instead is that he kissed me until my knees were weak and my lips were tender, and his uniquely warm, minty taste was permanently implanted in my brain. By that point, I had no real sense of where we were in the room, but he solved my unspoken question by effortlessly hefting me up, walking a few steps, and then lowering me onto the oversized bed, with our mouths still connected. Until they weren't.

Behind the mask, I opened my eyes to darkness as his lips grazed my jaw, then my chin, then my neck. Down and down he went, gifting me with soft wet things that half-suckle, half-kiss, and all appreciated. He cupped my breasts again, squeezing before he lowered his mouth, sucking my nipple through that soft lace. He did that for the other side too, then easily undid the front clasp of the bra, freezing my sensitive peaks to the open air.

The appreciative grunt he offered was the first sound he'd made since I told him I was staying, and it struck me as just as erotic as everything else. It didn't matter, but I closed my eyes as his mouth closed over my bare, hard nipples, with nothing to muffle the fullness of sensation now. And it was *glorious.*

Instinctively, I reached out, stopping when my fingers came in contact with his head. I couldn't see him, but nothing said I couldn't *touch* him, so I went for it, somewhat satisfying my curiosity with yet another detail to fill in – *waves.* My palms spread over his low cut, feeling the ridges of his waves on top, and the gradual fading of the sides. The lining around his hairline felt superbly crisp, letting me know the haircut was recent.

Which led me to the – probably dangerous – assumption that... he'd gotten a fresh haircut for me.

My shoulders relaxed as he moved lower, taking his lips down to my ribs, then my belly button, making my stomach cave in anticipation. I felt the release in tautness as he unhooked the stockings from my garter belt, sucked in a breath when I felt his fingers at the waist of the panties.

He tugged down, and immediately, I lifted my lower half to let him remove those panties. Once again, I was barely breathing – barely believing this was happening. But then he spread my legs open, burying his face between them, leaving no doubt that it *absolutely* was.

A high-pitched *"Ahh!"* shot from my lips as he covered me with his hot mouth, doing... *something*... with his tongue that damn near sent me through the ceiling. He hooked his arms around my thighs, pressing in closer, with his whole face, as he went in, slurping, licking, sucking, devouring me like he was starved.

My hands slipped from his head, down to his ears, down to his collar – still buttoned, tie still around his neck. That was all I needed to complete my little fantasy visual, of a tall, dark, sexy man, greedily eating my pussy while he was still all buttoned up.

Why was that was such an enticing visual? I had no idea. But it certainly fueled my record-time rocket to an intense orgasm that didn't seem to be his end goal – in fact, the fresh wave of wetness it brought seemed to make him go harder, like he was determined to lick me clean – an ambition I certainly had no complaints against him attempting.

50

Especially when he hooked his fingers into me, stroking deep and slow on a quest to find just the right spot. When he found it, it brought another implosion – even more intense than the first, so good that I damn near screamed myself hoarse with pleasure.

My chest heaved as I tried to catch my breath when he finally pulled himself from between my legs. I expected to hear him undressing, maybe even the sound of a condom wrapper, but instead he brought his lips to mine again, plying me with a kiss so deep I didn't even care that his face was still messy with my juices.

It was welcome proof of what he'd done to me.

"I have to go," he murmured against my lips, making me feel a disappointment I hadn't expected. "Desiree will let you know when I want to see you again. And I *definitely* want to see you again. Okay?"

I just nodded, somehow unable to speak, even though I'd been perfectly able to vocalize my pleasure moments before.

"Did you enjoy yourself?" he asked – I could hear the smirk in his voice, and knew he was teasing, but I nodded again anyway as I felt him climb off the bed. "Good," he responded to my answer. "Then we won't have any issues next time, will we?"

I swallowed. "No."

"Good. When the phone rings, you can take off the mask. There are clothes in the closet, and a driver waiting for you downstairs."

He didn't say goodbye.

I heard him in the bathroom, undoubtedly washing himself up, but then, without saying anything, his footsteps were in the hall, traveling away. A few moments later, the phone rang, just once, and I snatched the mask off my head, wildly looking around.

I was alone.

Why wouldn't you be?

Taking a deep breath, I shook my head. My stocking-clad feet caught my attention, reminding me that they, and the garter belt they'd been attached to, were the only articles of clothing still on my body. My legs were still splayed out, nipples still hard, and I was definitely sitting in a wet spot of my own creation that had probably ruined the expensive duvet he'd spread me on top of.

I braced myself, waiting for shame to take hold.

It never came.

I didn't feel dirty or embarrassed, the way I'd expected to. I just felt... *good.*

Pulling myself out of bed, I stripped down for another shower, and then went searching for the clothes he'd told me were there. I expected a few things at most, just enough for me to get home without it looking like a walk of shame, but instead I found *clothes.*

Nice ass clothes.

Pretty, obviously expensive undergarments in the drawers, all in the right sizes – obviously based on the information I'd had to provide to Desiree. In the closet were jeans, tops, dresses, shoes, whatever I needed to go pretty much anywhere, from a formal event to a private beach.

But all I wanted was to go home.

I tamped down my kidlike excitement, choosing the simplest bra and panties, the most basic jeans, and a plain tee shirt. I had every intention of simply putting on the shoes I'd worn to *get* here to go home, but one when I picked them up, I noticed something I hadn't earlier.

What had previously been a bad scuff, had now worn into a damn hole.

That brought the embarrassment.

When I imagined my life in my thirties, it certainly hadn't been this – not being able to afford a decent pair of shoes. Sitting there in that luxurious suite, with a closet full of things intended for my use… I couldn't *force* myself to put on those shoes.

I tossed them in the trash bin.

And then I went into the closet to pick a different pair, since now I had something I hadn't had before, hadn't had in a very, very long time.

Options.

It didn't make sense not to use them.

"Well if it isn't *Mr. President* himself. Gone and give us a campaign speech nigga," Braxton teased, putting out a hand to slap mine as I joined him, his brother Lincoln, and my other friends – Kingston and Trei – for a dinner I'd strongly contemplated missing.

For one, Braxton and Kingston weren't the most "political campaign" friendly homeboys to have. Secondly… coming here had required that I leave Rowan spread out on that bed, after a not *nearly* long enough sample of just how sweet she was to my taste buds.

A sample that I'd *sorely* needed.

Reid Bennet for City Council had taken an ugly hit today.

I was up against an opponent that had age, experience, and friends in high places on their side. What I had was passion, energy, and the ability to talk my way out of – or into – nearly anything. Because of that, early data suggested that I had a fighting chance, with a younger generation of voters, but today,

I'd been hit with an uppercut than in the world of Vegas politics, I might not recover from.

My opponent's husband had a heart attack. And there, in a live stream from his hospital bedside, he'd stated a wish – played on *every fucking local news station* – to see his wife elected councilwoman while he was alive to see it.

That seat was good as hers.

While I was sitting in a long-ass, depressing-ass meeting about what we would do next, to save my campaign, all I could think about was *not* thinking about any of this shit. That city council seat was important to me, absolutely – I wanted to make *real* change for the people of this city. Not the tourists and billionaires than ran the strip, but the *people*. I wanted to make a difference.

I didn't want to be a politician.

I just thought it was necessary.

But the more I learned about the dirty politics, nepotism, and outright *crime* that actually ran this city – something that campaigning for a "real" office had shown me – I was less inclined to believe it. Still, if having the office would put me in a position to effect even the smallest change, I wanted to do it.

But I was tired.

I was *really* fucking tired.

Tired of the campaign bullshit, tired of putting on appearances. Tired of pretending to still be in love with a woman whose betrayal I'd discovered months ago, but couldn't really do shit about, because she was *the* Enid Grant, of the *Grants*, and their name meant a whole lot in this city. I couldn't drop her, because a single black man who'd lost his fiancée to another man wasn't a candidate people were going to vote for. She stuck around because there was political capital involved for her as well, through her father, who was running for state representative.

Couldn't have his whore of a daughter creating a messy scandal, messing with his chances of election, and if her ass messed things up for *me,* there would *absolutely* be a fucking scandal.

But I wasn't trying to think about that. All I wanted was an escape, and that was where Rowan had come in. I knew we weren't supposed to have our initial meeting for a few more days, but after the blow to my campaign, I couldn't help it.

I *needed* her.

And it had sure as hell been worth it.

"Surprised to see you out and among the living man," Kingston teased as I took the empty seat beside him, requesting a *Mauve* and coke from the server who'd appeared. "Expected you to be holed up somewhere, strategizing your next move after ol' Betty gave her husband a heart attack to make sure she won."

Shaking my head, I laughed. That was *exactly* why I'd come out. Couldn't have the city thinking I was somewhere huddling in a corner, licking my wounds.

"That's what I pay a campaign manager for," I told him, propping my elbows on the table. "And mine thinks that it's a good idea for me to be seen doing some good deeds – out and about in the neighborhood with regular people."

Trei chuckled. "Look around, Reid... you're not among regular people."

"Not right *now*," I explained, thanking the server as she handed me my requested drink. I took a sip, then looked around the table. "Whatever you planned to do tomorrow between two and four, cancel it. We're going to a softball game."

Four.

What in the world...?

I pulled down the brim of my hat, squinting against the sun as I looked out into the packed stands, trying to figure out where half of the crowd was coming from. The annual softball game usually got decent attendance, but from what I could tell from the field, we'd easily doubled last years' numbers. Turning, I glanced around until my eyes landed at the tents we had set up for food, and I frowned at the unusually long lines.

The extra people were a strain I wasn't sure we could handle.

Stifling a yawn, I took my attention back to the nearly finishing game. I hurried to clap for one of the kids as he came in for a home run, grinning as he passed the finish line and scored the points that won the game for his team.

I congratulated the team who won, consoled the team who didn't. Talked to parents and sisters and uncles and whoever else approached, but honestly? It was all a blur.

My thoughts were consumed by last night.

It had been late when I was dropped off at home, and frustratingly early when my alarm went off this morning, waking me from not nearly enough sleep. I'd closed my eyes thinking about "Mr. President". Dreamed about him. Woken up with him on my mind.

The things your first orgasm after a drought will do to you.

56

I must have still been looking dazed when Mila walked up, practically bubbling with excitement.

"What's wrong with you? You look lost," she said, hooking her arm through mine. "You have to perk up, and quickly – do you see this crowd, and all these cameras?!"

I blinked, realizing that she was right – I'd definitely noticed the crowd already, but now that I was away from the field closer to the building, there *were* cameras and vans on the other side of the fence.

News cameras.

Local, but still.

"Yeah, I do. You wanna tell me what this is about?" I asked, hoping she had the answers I didn't. But instead of the explanation I was looking for, what I got was wide-eyed confusion.

"Huh? You didn't arrange this?" Mila raised an eyebrow. "Here I thought that this was what Desiree spirited you away last night for. Signing non-disclosures or something in exchange for getting these big name donors here."

I reared my head back. "I'm sorry, what? What big name donors?"

Mila sighed. "Okay now boss lady, I'm going to give you a pass since I know you've been crazy busy this morning with last-minute logistics and then coaching the game. But next time my future ex-husband Braxton Drake is in attendance at a Cartwright Center event, I *really* need you to take notice," she teased, pulling my arm to get me to follow her.

"Wait a minute – *Braxton Drake* is here?!" I squealed as she pulled me through the lines of people waiting for food, back into the building.

"Along with his fine ass twin and fine ass friends," Mila tossed over her shoulder as she led me out the side door to the playground, past all-black clad security that I didn't recognize, and certainly wasn't *ours*.

There were a lot of people out here too, but not enough that there wasn't room for the kids to play. The elementary kids were all over the jungle gym and swings, toddlers taking advantage of several kiddie pools and sprinklers set up in the grass, and some of the older kids were hooping on the basketball courts, which were badly in need of repair.

My attention moved to a small crowd of reporters with their phones and other cameras out, snapping pictures of the whole scene, which made me take a second look and realize something was out of place.

Those weren't *just* kids out there.

With wide eyes, I counted multiple members of what my regular-ass friends and I referred to as Las Vegas black royalty. Kingston Whitfield and Braxton Drake were playing basketball and talking trash with my teenagers. Lincoln Drake and Nashira Haley were tossing water balloons with middle-schoolers. Asha Davis, poker star, Kingston Whitfield's fiancée, baby bump and all, was pushing a laughing kindergartener on the swings while her bodyguard stood close by.

And those were just the "celebrity" names.

I recognized prominent business owners who I'd called before, leaving messages with their secretaries begging for donations only to be ignored – some of the very same ones who'd left me jaded about going after those types anyway.

For some reason, they were *all* here today.

Don't look a gift horse in the mouth, Rowan.

I'd never really "gotten" the expression, but I got the sentiment. I was fully prepared to just be grateful for the attention and hope they'd all brought their checkbooks when I realized they all had more than just *money* in common.

58

They were all wearing *Reid Bennett for City Council* buttons.

And just like that, I went from grateful to livid.

It was *just* like some local politician to turn something that was supposed to be about these kids, about preserving this center, this community into a goddamn campaign event.

"Mila," I hissed, pulling her closer to me. "Who the *fuck* is Reid Bennett, and who gave him permission to turn my softball game into a damn campaign rally?"

My eyes darted around, following the largest group of reports to where they'd made a circle around someone I couldn't quite see because of the all the people and cameras. It wasn't that I was completely clueless about politics – I'd purposely chosen to divest. At its prime, the *Cartwright Center* had been the proud recipient of grants and other government funding that kept it thriving. But over time, as certain offices filled with one corrupt politician after another, that funding had dwindled to practically nothing. People campaigned on hope-filled promises that they didn't keep, and I'd lost the little faith I had.

I would keep applying for grants and whatever other resources were being offered, but other than that? I just focused on keeping this center running. When it seemed like the worst crook always ended up being the winner, it was much easier to just ignore the whole system versus willingly signing up for political heartbreak.

But now, it was right on my front door.

Reid Bennett had a *lot* of nerve.

Where the hell had he been before now? Certainly not writing checks to keep this place open, or offering a letter of recommendation for my grant application, or hell – at least *asking* if I were okay with him using this place to boost his public image.

"He's running for City Council," Mila explained, then held up a hand as annoyance crossed my face. *And* he's engaged to Enid Grant."

"Of *the* Grants?" I asked, rolling my eyes. I'd gone to high school with Enid for exactly one year, by virtue of a private school tuition voucher I'd won through a program at a local college. I didn't even apply for a second voucher, preferring to take my chances at public school instead of waiting to be victimized by spoiled rich kids like Enid and the rest of her little crowd.

Enid was horrible back then, and from the tabloid stories about her over the years, she still was. If Reid Bennett was marrying *her*, it told me just about everything I needed to know.

"Yeah," Mila confirmed. "*Those* Grants. He's losing in the polls though, unfortunately."

I smirked. "Is that why he's doing this? Too lame to get votes by going about it a better way?"

"He's actually not lame at all." Mila's lips spread into a little smile. "He has quite a bit of swag, actually. Very handsome, educated without coming off like a know-it-all, charming. No scandals, no wild shit. He's a pretty prime candidate."

"Then why is he losing?"

Mila sighed. "Because he's a young black man with little to no political experience, and his opponent is a white, female doctor, whose husband just had a heart attack. He gets on live TV yesterday and says he wants to see his wife in that seat before he "goes on to glory"."

"Oh *damn*," I cringed. "No wonder Mr. Bennet is trying to get some support going. He probably picked the blackest event he could find on the city calendar."

"That's a strong possibility," Mila agreed. "But, look at all the free publicity we've gotten. All the concession sales, plus donation checks..."

"The checks don't mean anything until they clear the bank," I said, shaking my head. "And donations don't excuse the fact that his presence here implies an endorsement."

Mila grabbed my hand, squeezing my fingers. "Don't overthink it, Ro. It's a good day. Just enjoy it."

"Ugh. I guess," I conceded with a sigh. "I'm sending a strongly worded email to his campaign though. I don't appreciate being used like this."

"You do that," Mila laughed. "And in the meantime, look around at all these happy faces. Celebrity takeover aside, you've pulled off another great event."

"Uh-huh. I know these folks better write some fat checks," I fussed, making her laugh again – laughter that stopped rather abruptly. When I looked up to see why, my breath caught in my throat.

Damn he's fine.

I had to remind myself to close my mouth, to avoid looking quite so easily impressed by smooth chocolate skin and nice biceps.

"Excuse me ladies – I was hoping your *Cartwright Center* shirts meant I could seek some assistance you," he started, looking back and forth between Mila and me, before he let his gaze linger on mine. "I have several very upset four-year-olds wanting to know why the bubble machine stopped working."

I frowned. "Oh – I didn't even know we had a bubble machine. I wouldn't know where to begin with fixing it."

He flashed a smile, showing off nice white teeth. "I'm pretty sure we're just out of the mixture we need. And uh, I should probably clarify. *I'm* the bubble machine," he explained, touching my arm as he finished.

"*Oh*," I giggled, not at all bothered by his touch. "Well, your services are appreciated, Mr....?"

"Perry. Jeff Perry. I work with WAWG. Just opened a Vegas location for the network, and they want to try their hand at the news, so here I am," he said, extending a hand, which I accepted. "I'd heard of the Cartwright Center before, but I'm sorry to say this is my first visit. Definitely won't be the last though," he told me, still holding my hand, which he squeezed, sending a little flash of electricity through me, making me blush.

"Well, better late than never, right?" I smiled. "We are certainly very glad to have the city's attention. Finally."

He nodded. "Absolutely. So... about those bubbles?"

"Oh! Right. We have more, in the recreation closet. I can go grab them. I'll be right back," I said, already moving as I spoke the last word.

"I can just follow you," he called after me, quickly catching up.

I stopped moving to meet his eyes, and almost immediately got swallowed by their chocolatey depths. "Uh... yeah. Yeah, four hands can hold more than two I guess."

I pushed out a little breath, suddenly feeling self-conscious about my sweaty tee shirt and faded shorts. I'd dressed this morning with comfort and coolness in mind – not hot men and photo ops.

Not that you could do anything about this hot man anyway, I reminded myself. For the length of my contract, I wasn't supposed to be dating, so it wasn't like I could do anything about my attraction to Jeff anyway.

With that in mind, I turned my dial from giggly teenager back to professional as I led Jeff to the room we used as storage for a wide assortment of things. I used my key to unlock the door, then held it open for him as I flipped the switch to get the lights on.

"Well, *wow*," he exclaimed, stopping at the door instead of venturing further. "This is a lot."

I laughed, looking around at what he probably saw as a mess. The room was filled with tall shelves, holding everything from boxes of jump ropes to tennis balls to horseshoe games, and it was packed tight, but everything had a place.

"Yeah, it is, but I know exactly where the bubbles are," I called, knowing he couldn't see me once I stepped into one of the aisles. "There's an art to this!"

"That doesn't surprise me to hear you say that," he responded, laughing. "From what I read, seems like you run this place like a well-oiled machine."

I shook my head as I picked up four big bottles of bubble mix, and headed back to him. "I don't know about *well* oiled. We could definitely use as much *oil* as we can get – so I hope you brought your checkbook too, Mr... wait – did you just say that you'd read about me? So you already knew who I was?"

I stepped back into the open with my arms full of bubbles, brows furrowed as I waited for him to respond. He gave me a sheepish grin that only made him more handsome.

"I... uh... just a little. After we got the email from Reid this morning."

My eyebrows unwrinkled, moving upward instead. "Email from Reid? What email?"

"Just a little encouragement to show some support to a community event. Nothing official. He's been wanting to do a few lowkey things to meet his constituents, and this was perfect. He hit up a few friends and acquaintances to show some support as well."

"So you're what… friend or acquaintance?"

"An active member of the community who is interested in the political landscape. Just keeping an eye out."

"By helping Reid Bennet with his unauthorized takeover of my annual softball game. Noted," I told him, dumping the bottles of bubble mixture into his arms. I went back to grab a few more, then breezed past him into the hall. "Come on. The door will automatically lock behind us."

"Why do I feel like I've offended you somehow," Jeff asked, easily catching up to my quick footsteps because of his long legs.

I glanced back at him as we made our way outside. "I'm not offended. I'm annoyed."

He moved in front of me, stopping me from getting any further in the thick crowd. "Is there a difference?"

"I don't know," I shrugged. "Still processing."

Jeff nodded. "Well, for what it's worth, Reid's heart is in the right place, I think, unlike a lot of these other politicians. He's not immune to the bullshit that comes along with it – nobody is. But… I believe him when he says he wants to better for our community."

"Yeah, well…" I pushed out a breath. "Maybe he could've started by reaching out, doing this the right way. The *Cartwright Center* is small, and broke. As you can see, we're working on limited resources, and I really could've used a heads up before he decided to make this a campaign stop. I'm grateful for the publicity, but I'm more than a little pissed that we got blindsided."

"Which isn't unreasonable," Jeff agreed, nodding again. "But for what it's worth – again, you seem to be doing a great job. I see a lot of smiling faces and happy kids."

My shoulders relaxed a bit as I let a grin break free. "Yeah… I guess you're right. And I also guess that the bubble machine needs to be back in commission ASAP. I'm pretty sure I'm watching the beginnings of a mob of disgruntled four-year-olds over there."

He laughed. "Yeah, I think you're right. So… shall we?"

My eyes went a little wide as the suggestion of joining him, but the warmth of his smile made it easy to nod.

"Yeah, I guess we shall."

As soon as we stepped into the area, the kids went wild, mobbing him over the bubbles. He was a good – no, *great* – sport about it, laughing and teasing as he cracked open a fresh bottle of solution and went to town.

I passed out bottles to a few other volunteers, and soon the whole area was thick with bubbles that the kids were all too eager to chase and pop. Inevitably, my eyes kept going back to Jeff, watching the loving, warm way that he interacted.

Why did I never meet men like this when I wasn't beholden to a goddamn sex contract?

Feeling eyes on *me*, I looked up and around, only to have my gaze land on Desiree Byers. She looked from me to Jeff and then smirked, turning to disappear into the crowd after completely freaking me out.

What the hell was that smirk about?

As I returned my gaze to Jeff, it occurred to me that he was similar to *Mr. President* in both skin tone and build. For a wild moment, I wondered if…

No way, Rowan. Absolutely not.

Jeff Perry was… a journalist or something, if he was helping set up a local news office. Why in the world would he need a level of secrecy like what was involved in that contract? Would he even have the money to meet the terms of it? And why would he openly make conversation and flirt with me, after making all those provisions in our contract?

No… there was no way.

Unless he just gets off on this…

Frantically, I searched my brain for any other context clues that Jeff Perry had been the man treating my pussy like a dying man's last meal the night before. The body type and skin tone were right, but what else?

Was his voice the same?

Did he smell the same?

Is that why I'd been so comfortable with him touching me a moment ago?

Is that why Desiree was smirking?

I was so busy wracking my mind trying to figure this out I barely noticed that *now*, I had several sets of eyes on me – reporters, from when I'd first come out. The crowd that had been around who I assumed was Reid Bennet had thinned out, enough for me to see the man himself as he pointed at me, saying something that had shifted the media attention in my direction.

Before I knew it, it was *me* who was surrounded, being asked questions about the center. Overwhelmed, I searched for Mila in the area around me, but she was nowhere to be found, which meant I was on my own. My eyes landed on Jeff, only to find him staring back, with a smile and nod.

I took a deep breath, and then slapped on a smile of my own.

An impromptu interview was nothing I couldn't handle.

66

Today's event at the Cartwright Center went off without a hitch, even with the unexpectedly large crowd brought on by City Council candidate Reid Bennett's surprise appearance. Reid brought along some of his billionaire friends, whose names attracted more of a crowd than the center is used to. The community seemed happy for their presence as they jumped right into basketball games and water balloon fights to display a down-to-earth side we rarely see from what the media has dubbed "Las Vegas Black Royalty".

There was one person, however, who was less than impressed.

Rowan Phillips, taken in at a young age by Janie Cartwright, is now the director of the center, and the main organizer of the festivities. She was overheard saying that she felt blindsided by Bennet's unscheduled drop-in, and wished she had been given an opportunity to better prepare. When directly interviewed, however, Ms. Phillips was much more neutral.

"I told you she wouldn't like it," Des fussed, as soon as I looked up from reading the article that had appeared online this morning, on none other than WAWG's news site.

I hadn't had a great feeling about it when Des warned the day before that Jeff Perry was sniffing around Rowan, but this confirmed it, at least in my mind.

He was getting in the way of what I already considered mine.

"I bet she liked the half mil she racked up in donations," I countered, tossing my phone onto the desk in front of me. "I did her a favor."

Des shook her head. "But you certainly did none for yourself. She made enough in donations that it's probably looking pretty enticing to her to simply break your little contract."

"She's smart enough to know that the ongoing terms I offered are worth more than that," I said. "Five hundred thousand is nice, but we both know her ambitions. The things she wants to do, the kids she wants to reach. Trust me, she's not backing out."

"She almost backed out *without* half a million dollars in the bank, remember?" Des said, making me wish I hadn't shared that particular tidbit with her. It was important that she knew though – especially since Rowan had taken that mask off, and had seen my hands, at the very least.

"I talked her down. She's cool."

"And what about when Jeff Perry talks her down. To her knees. And puts his dick down her throat. Because you know that's what he wants, right? And from the way he had her halfway swooning, he'll probably get it, and during their pillow talk after, she'll share how she signed a little contract, and—"

"She's *not* going to break the contract," I insisted, sitting up and looking Des right in the eyes. "She knows not to let anything happen with him."

"While she's under contract? Sure. But what about after?"

"She won't break that non-disclosure," I told Des, with full confidence in my words. "She's going to see this article on Jeff's site and know that anything she says to him is fair game for the whole world to hear about."

Des shook her head. "He didn't write the article."

"But he let her *obviously* off-the-record words go to print, knowing that the "neutral" response she gave the reporters was what she wanted to be public."

Across from me, Des' eyebrows went up. "Okay. Fair point. But *still* – this highlights part of why this was always a dangerous idea to me. Rowan is smart as hell, very ambitious, attractive… all of which makes her a viable prospect to the upper echelon of black bachelors in this city who didn't even know she existed until *you* put this spotlight on her. Your pockets are *not* the deepest ones around here, Reid. I'm telling you – it's going to take more than that to keep her in your bed."

"Well," I smirked. "It's a good thing I have more than that to offer." I sat back and closed my eyes, thinking about the sweetness of her pussy in my face again, knowing there was still so much more left to experience. "Call her," I said, eyes still closed.

"What should I tell her?"

"To have her ass back in that hotel room tonight. I'm going to make sure any nigga that comes after me has to feel my imprint when he's inside of her."

Des let out a little squeal, that made me open my eyes to find her elbows propped on the desk as she smiled.

"Now *that* is the kind of thing I want to hear," she gushed. "I thought politics had ruined you. Glad to see that isn't the case."

"Ruined me?" I asked as she stood, gathering her things to leave my office.

She nodded. "You've changed, love. The Grants... they've changed you."

"You know what that's about, Des."

"I do. But still. I hope it's worth it."

"So do I."

"I hope Rowan makes you remember yourself."

I pushed out a sigh, knowing exactly what Des meant, but having little interest in acknowledging it. At least not for now.

"Then make sure she's available for me," I told Des, keeping my tone gentle, even as my patience grew thin.

Des smiled.

"Yeah. Dialing now."

Five.

"Knock-knock."

The sound of a male voice in the doorway to my office jolted me from my work, shifting my "lost-in-what-I-was-doing" status to "lost-in-those-eyes".

Jeff Perry was *fine*.

Unbidden, my heart started beating a little faster as a smile drifted across his lips and he stepped into the office, hands tucked into his slacks.

"Ms. Phillips… what a pleasure to lay eyes on you again," he said, taking it upon himself to occupy the seat in front of my desk – a liberty that reminded me I was annoyed with him.

And impossibly intrigued.

"I'm not sure yet if I can say the same, Mr. Perry," I replied, laying down the pen I'd been using so that I could prop my chin in my hands. "Perry, as in, *Nubia* Perry, as in, Nubia Perry's "favorite cousin", as in… not "just" a journalist, as you let me assume. You don't *work* for the Las Vegas WAWG affiliate station – you *run* it," I told him, wanting to be sure he knew that *I* knew he'd left a few details out.

My words made him grin, and sit back in the chair with his legs spread wide. "I see you've done your research."

"Well, after my off-the-record words appeared in your publication and are now being used against Reid Bennet's campaign, I figured I should probably find out *exactly* who I was blowing bubbles with."

He raised an eyebrow. "Oh? You read a couple of news articles and think you know me?"

"Not in the slightest," I countered. "I understand the difference between the story the media tells and the truth. Do you?

"Oh damn," he chuckled. "That sounded like a jab. Felt like one too."

"And you sound like a hit dog hollering," I told him, raising an eyebrow. "What can I do for you Mr. Perry?"

At that, he sat forward, leaning toward the desk. "You can give me the pleasure of having you on my arm at the Armstrong Gala."

This time, it was *my* eyebrows that hiked up, remaining perched near my hairline as I reminded him, "The Armstrong Gala is next week, and the guest list is exclusive – harder to get into than… one of Kingston Whitfield's poker games," I said, using a reference I only had a vague knowledge of, but thought it fit right into Jeff's social status. "And my name is most certainly absent."

"You say that like it matters."

"Are you saying it doesn't?"

He shrugged, with an arrogant smirk that made me have to shift a little in my seat. "For me… not much. If you're on my arm, your entry is guaranteed."

"So you're what, an A-lister?" I asked.

"Your phrase, not mine," he grinned. "So what do you say? Accompany me to this event, rub elbows with Vegas' "Black Royalty", maybe secure a few donations. Get to know me better than those articles you read…"

I laughed. "Sounds like quite a night."

"I certainly intend to make it so. So…?"

I pushed out a sigh. "I… uhh…"

"Don't tell me you've got a man," he groaned, making me laugh as I shook my head. "No? A woman then?" he shrugged again. "That's fine. I don't mind competition."

"I don't have a woman," I giggled, then immediately calmed myself as I considered my situation. "There is someone whose... counsel... I would need to seek, before I said yes."

He waved a hand, brushing me off. "*Oh.* Who, your homegirls or something? Friends always love me."

"You realize that isn't necessarily a perk, don't you?"

"You realize that depends on the woman and the friends, don't you?"

My brows dropped. "Oooh, okay," I laughed. "But no, not my friends either. Just... someone. It's complicated."

"I'm a man who can take no for an answer, Rowan."

"That's nice, but I'm not saying *no.* I'm saying that I have to get back to you."

He nodded, staring at me for a moment before he pushed up from the chair, digging out his wallet for a card to put on my desk. "My number. Office and personal cell. Let me know, okay?"

"Thank you for the offer," I told him with a smile. "I absolutely will."

After that, he turned and left, leaving my mind running with possibilities – a state that didn't last very long before my cell phone rang, drawing my attention away.

I frowned when I saw Desiree Byers' name on the screen. *Were they spying on me?*

Briefly – *very* briefly – I entertained the idea of not answering the phone, but common sense ruled over that.

"Hello Ms. Byers," I answered, as pleasantly as I could. "To what do I owe the pleasure of your call?"

72

On the other end of the line, she laughed. "No need for the all formalities," she said. "Keep all of it, actually. It's just Des. And I think you know why I'm calling."

I sighed. "Yes. Of course."

"You don't sound very excited – do you have some feedback you need me to give the client? I'm quite sure he'd want to know if you were unhappy."

I shook my head, though she couldn't see me. "No. It's not that, I just… I think I expected a little more time. A break, I guess."

"Do you need a break?"

"I… I suppose not. He wants to see me tomorrow?"

"He wants to see you *today*. And he wants that to not be a problem."

Rolling my eyes, I thought about the sushi I was supposed to be having with Laurel and a few other homegirls tonight. It wasn't unheard of for one of us to cancel – it wasn't even that big of a deal for one of us to cancel over a guy.

Me canceling over a guy whose face I'd never even seen… that was definitely outside of the trend.

"Then… I guess it isn't. What time should I be ready?"

"A car will be waiting to take you to the hotel at eight tonight. You should already be showered and dressed in the attire my client has provided by the time he arrives at nine."

I glanced at my watch. It was already approaching five, and I still had work to do. Not wanting to alarm Des, I held the urge to let out another sigh, swallowing my agitation instead. Honestly… thinking back on what had happened between us a few days ago, there was no reason for me to dread my time with her "client".

"Okay. I guess it's a date."

Shit, shit, shit!

I hurried from the car, barely giving it time to come to a full stop before I flung myself out. My footsteps were quick, not even allowing myself time to feel out of place in my yoga pants and tank top.

I was late.

I *hated* being late.

I bounced on the balls of my feet in the simple flats I'd tossed on, growing more and more impatient as I waited for the elevator. It wasn't *my* fault that it was already ten minutes after nine – we'd gotten stuck right behind a car accident that brought traffic to a standstill for over an hour – but I had no way of knowing if that was an acceptable excuse.

Had no way of knowing how "Nick" would feel about being kept waiting.

In my defense, I'd tried to call Desiree, but hadn't gotten an answer. I'd left a message and texted her too, explaining what was happening, but still hadn't received a response. I had *no* idea what I was walking into.

Maybe he isn't here yet, I told myself, hoping beyond hope that *maybe* that was true. It was a big city, and traffic caused delays all the time. And there was no doubt he was a busy man. Maybe a meeting had run late, or he was stuck on a conference call, or… hell, *anything* that would give me even a little bit more time to get myself ready for me.

I was thanking my lucky stars that I'd showered at home, so at least that was taken care of. I'd planned to run a flat iron through my hair once I arrived at the hotel, but with time no longer on my side, I stepped onto the elevator when it *finally* arrived, and had my hands up, unraveling one of my French braids as the doors closed.

I'd done those braids after a thorough wash following the softball game, and hadn't touched them since. Now, using the mirrored walls of the elevator, I ran my fingers through the uniform crinkles the braids had left behind, giving myself big, fluffy hair that rested around my shoulders like a mane, making me look sexier than I felt.

As soon as the elevator doors opened, I sprinted down the hall, digging in my bag for the keycard I'd gotten from the driver. The little green light on the door blinked, and then the locks disengaged, allowing me to enter. Once I was on the other side of the closed door, I realized the suite was still mostly dark, which meant Nick hadn't made it. I pressed my back against the door in relief, taking just a second to catch my breath before I stepped forward to make my way to the bedroom to get dressed.

"Stop right there," I heard, as soon as my feet crossed the bedroom threshold.

My hand shot up to my chest as if it would stop my heart from slamming out of my chest the way it wanted to. With wide eyes, I scanned the dark bedroom for the source of the words in vain. At least, until my eyes adjusted to the dark.

There, in the corner, just *barely* illuminated by the light coming through the window, he sat. I could only make out his outline – the sharp curve of his chin, ears that were *just* a little too big, the slope of his haircut before the next demand came.

"Close your eyes, Rowan. No peeking."

My eyes shut when he said it, so quickly that it felt like he was more in charge of my body than I was. Logically, I knew that the driver had probably alerted him that I was on my way up, that it was unlikely he'd been sitting in the dark, but something about the pitch blackness I found myself surrounded by made the hair stand up on my arms.

It didn't help that there was a sudden, resounding clink of glass hitting wood, followed by the distinct shuffle of clothes across leather. He was standing, and staring, and stalking toward me in slow, deliberate steps across the carpet. I expected him to say something once he reached me, but the only thing I got was continued silence as he tied the blindfold over my face, weaving it through my hair in a way that kept it flowing free and wild.

"I'm sorry I'm late," I said, blindly pointing my head in the direction where I felt his warmth. "There was—"

"An accident. I know." His tone was clipped – not necessarily out of annoyance, but definitely impatience, which didn't make my heart beat any less rapid. I shivered as he slipped a hand underneath my tank top, underneath the cami bra I wore, to caress my breast. "You already showered?" he asked, pressing closer to me, pressing my back against the wall beside the door.

Just as I opened my mouth to answer, he put his mouth to my neck, sucking my skin just hard enough to make me cringe in pain before I felt the rasp of his tongue, soothing my tender flesh.

"I…*yes*," I breathed, hoping he understood it was an answer and a request. He must have gotten it, because he did it again, cupping and squeezing my breast as he did. I whimpered as his teeth grazed my neck, teasing before he bit down – another gratifying twinge he calmed with his tongue.

"Good."

That one-word warning was all I got before his other hand was in my panties, between my legs, thumb pressed against my clit as two fingers invaded my wetness. My mouth fell open, taken aback by his abruptness but also turned on by it. I opened my legs to give him better access, and tilted my head back for the same reason, moaning and sighing in response to his tongue on my neck.

But then suddenly, instead of at my neck, his mouth was on mine and his hand was buried in my hair, pulling me into a deep, bruising sort of kiss. I didn't even think about it before I tossed my arms around his neck, rocking my hips into his hand as he stroked me with his fingers.

His tongue took residence in my mouth, tasting and teasing and leaving behind the oaky-sweet flavor of whatever had been in the glass I heard him put down. His thick fingers pushed deeper, bringing forth a hot coil of pleasure I'd always considered elusive, but seemed so easily attainable with him.

In next to no time, I was on the verge of exploding. Nick unraveled his hand from my hair long enough to tug my tank top and bra down, exposing my breasts to the cool, dark air. A harsh moan ripped from my throat as he bent his head to suck my nipple into his mouth, tugging it with his teeth. My hands moved from his shoulders to his head, holding him in place as he licked and sucked the overly sensitive peak until I was shaking.

Between his mouth and his fingers, I felt him all over – the pleasurable prickling of my skin, the throbbing of my breasts, the contractions between my legs signaling that I was ready for more than just his hand, I was ready for *him*.

Propping my hands on either side of his head, I drew him back upward, sightlessly pressing my mouth to his. Once he took over the kiss I dropped my hands, sliding them down over the hard plane of his chest, down to his stomach, down to his belted slacks.

There, I froze.

Was I really about to do this?

In front of me, Nick had stopped moving too, and the pause in activity allowed a moment of clarity to creep through. Him going down on me was one thing – one scandalous thing I could never publicly admit. Actual factual intercourse was another.

That was crossing a whole different line I wasn't sure I was ready for.

Should've thought about that before you signed the paperwork.

I swallowed, hard.

Yes, Desiree Byers had made it clear that this was something I could walk away from. I could even leave with some of my perks intact – enough perks to at least survive the rest of the year, with some left over. I didn't *have* to do this – not out of fear, not for money. But the thing was… at this point… I *wanted* to do it, as embarrassing as that was.

Not embarrassing enough to make me stop though.

I snapped back into action, unbuttoning and unzipping and tugging until my hands made contact with his painfully hard erection. Just to myself, I smiled a little at his sharp intake of breath when I wrapped my hand around it, squeezing as I pumped him just enough to get an idea of his size.

Before my brain could process what I was feeling, he'd pulled away, yanking me away from the wall. I gasped a little as he tossed me across the bed, roughly ridding me of my yoga pants and panties before he pulled me up on my knees, pushed my upper half down until I was perched on my hands, and then plunged into me from behind.

Long, and thick.

There was my answer.

I didn't even try to muffle my screams of pleasure – I let it *all* out as he drove into me, burying himself as deep as my body would allow, over, and over, and over again. His arm went around my waist, anchoring me in place as he dug in, hitting every nook and cranny before he pulled back and then repeated himself.

I closed my eyes because it was the only thing I *could* do as his strokes grew faster, and the wetter I got, deeper. The harder he fucked me, the lower my upper half dropped, until nothing but my ass was in the air, my cheeks serving as hand grips as he stroked me into a moaning, screaming mess on the bed.

I didn't think it was possible for me to cum harder than I during our first rendezvous, but he proved me wrong. I came in a flood of static and color, so loud and bright that I was temporarily void of my senses, but then it all came rushing back, in a wave of pleasure that made me scream myself hoarse.

It was really, *realllyyy* good.

The type of good that I didn't think could possibly get better until he flipped me over, settling between my legs to sink into me again after he'd gotten rid of the rest of our clothes. Instead of pounding into me, chasing his own nut, he went… slow.

Deliciously slow.

All my nerve endings were raw – still in a tizzy from that orgasm. So everything about this – from the feeling of his hips locked between my thighs, to the rasp of skin on skin, to his hand on my neck, to the sweat dripping from his brow to mine – was amplified. It was so good that I barely felt like I was in my own body until he brought his mouth to mine, for another liquor-infused kiss that brought me back to earth.

I didn't know what more to do than wrap my arms around him, sinking my nails into his back as he sank into me, filling me to a point that felt like too much and not enough, at once. A whimper left my throat with each stroke, and my hands moved lower as my whimpers came faster, until I was leaving nail prints in his ass cheeks as he settled into a steady rhythm.

My legs constricted around him as my back arched, pressed up toward him as he pressed down into me. That hot coil of pleasure started building again, tighter and hotter as the tension rose in his hips. My mouth opened and never closed, sucking in whatever breath I could as Nick buried his face in my neck. This time when I came, it was accompanied by a soundless scream, and then a loud, harsh, guttural growl into my neck from him as he came, slamming so hard that I was sure we'd be stuck together long after he was finished emptying himself into me.

There was no point in opening my eyes behind the mask, so I didn't. The multiple orgasms had wrung every last bit of energy I had after a long day at work, so I didn't bother trying to move at all.

Neither did he.

And after a few moments, the weight of his body on top of mine lulled me to sleep.

I may have fucked up.

The longer I laid there, watching Rowan sleep, the more apparent it became that "may have" was more like "definitely".

Her mask had slipped off, but instead of fixing it, or getting my ass out of there before she woke up and saw my face, I was just… watching.

She was too beautiful not to.

80

Now that I'd watched her, felt her come unglued around my dick, I wanted her even more. Nevermind that I *had* her. I still wanted her. Wanted more.

More than the terms of my ill-advised contract could provide.

Here was a woman who was everything – smart, resourceful, kind, sexy as hell – that I wanted. I had her in my bed. Well… in *a* bed.

And yet, she was still out of my reach.

The buzzing of my cell phone caught my attention, and I reluctantly pulled my gaze away from the nude, sex-drained goddess in front of me. The name on the screen immediately made my eyes roll, but I pulled myself up from my seat, knowing Enid wouldn't stop calling until she had my attention.

The woman was a master at snatching peaceful moments away from me.

Knowing it was time for me to go, I approached the bed, standing over Rowan for one last time for the night. She stirred a little in her sleep and I didn't move, recklessly concluding that if she opened her eyes, I'd just have to accept it.

She didn't.

She settled back into the covers, so peaceful and beautiful that it made it hard as fuck to leave. But I had to. So I bent to press a kiss to her lips, feeling a deep pang of regret when that soft peck made her mouth curve into a subconscious smile.

That made me get my ass out of that hotel room.

Yeah.

I fucked up.

Six.

"So what did he say when you asked him about going to the gala with Jeff?"

I stopped with a grape halfway up to my mouth to frown at Laurel, who was sitting across from me at my kitchen counter. "Girl, I just told you I barely got two words out of my mouth before the man had his hands in my panties. What, exactly, makes you think I made time to ask that man if I could be on someone else's arm at a gala?"

"Lucky bitch," Laurel snickered, then picked up a cube of cheese. "Why doesn't stuff like this ever happen to me? I like wild hotel sex too."

Shaking my head, I frowned at her again. "You're joking, right? You're not seriously jealous of my sex contract with a stranger are you?"

"Hell yeah I am," she said, sucking her teeth. "He sounds fine as hell. And then you have Jeff Perry sweating you too, and we *know* he looks good. It's honestly not fair. You have too many niggas, while I don't have enough."

I laughed. "Laurel, *bye*. First of all, I don't have *any*. And second, you're not about to front like you don't curve men left and right."

"But we're not talking about that right now though. You have two fine ass men who want you – what are you gonna do?"

"Not a single thing any different than what I'm already doing," I explained. "You see two men who want me – I see two men who want to fuck me, one of whom is already paying for the privilege of doing so."

"You mean, one of whom wanted it so bad he signed a contract for that pussy," Laurel sang, doing a little jig on her

82

barstool that made me laugh. "And yeah, of course Jeff wants to fuck you, but *so what*? It would happen eventually if you two were dating anyway, so…"

"That's a *huge* if. I don't know him like that, and can't really *get* to know him for another three weeks – not until the contract is done. I'm only entertaining the gala because I think it would be good for the center for me to get some face time with potential donors."

"*Ugh*," Laurel groaned. "It always comes back to the center for you, doesn't it?"

I shrugged. "Yeah, and?"

"*And*, you're still young and fine! All you ever do is work at the center, or worry about the center, or talk about the center. When is the last time you did something just for Rowan?"

Rolling my eyes at where the conversation was heading, I picked up my wine glass for a sip – partially because I need the alcohol to dull my senses, and partially because I needed something to delay having to give an answer.

Last night had *definitely* felt "just for Rowan", but… now that I was outside of the moment and looking back, it didn't feel right to say that.

Not that I thought I'd be judged – this was Laurel, there was very little I could say to make her look down on, or think less of me. It was less about saying it to someone than it was about admitting it to myself.

Admitting that not so deep down… I was enjoying this.

"Those kids need me – need *this*," was what I said out loud, not ready to have that transparent conversation quite yet. It was so much easier to bring it back around to the kids, as if that were the only reason I'd gone to that hotel room last night. "For most of them, the people at the center are the only ones who can or will drop everything for them. The center is a lifeline, and I

refuse to let it fail. Even if it means sacrificing my social life…
for now."

Laurel sighed. "I get it, Ro. I really do. I just don't want
to see you burn yourself out working on everything but yourself.
You deserve too. That's why I'm no glad to hear that Mystery
Nigga has been putting in work, making sure you get yours.
You'd better see if you can sign a contract extension or
something. A month of orgasms is *not* enough."

"It is *plenty*," I argued, laughing.

"Girl whatever. Since that's the case, you send him my
way next then, okay?"

"I'll see what I can do."

"You do that," Laurel implored as she stood. "Wait
though – you don't think it's Obama, do you?"

I almost choked on the sip of water I'd been taking.
"*What*?" I sputtered. "*No*, it is *not* goddamn Obama!"

"How do you know?!"

"I told you, I saw his skin tone the first day. He's dark
chocolate."

Laurel nodded. "Oh, okay good. Cause Michelle is my
girl, and I wasn't trying to have to fight my bestie over my
forever first lady's man."

"Weren't you leaving? Can we still make that happen?"

She put a hand to her chest. "Wow, so are you putting me
out now though?"

"Yes, I am," I laughed. "Because it is still early enough
for me to do something *just for Rowan* before I go to bed."

"Rub one out?"

"If by that you mean fall asleep before I finish one
episode of my current Netflix binge, then yes. I'm gonna rub the
hell out of it."

84

Laurel was still laughing when she left, and my own great mood persisted as I headed back to the kitchen to clean up. It wasn't much to do – just putting away the things we'd been snacking on and wiping the counter down before I could make my way to the living room to plop down on the couch.

I'd been there maybe ten minutes when my phone buzzed, and I picked it up to find a text from Laurel letting me know she'd made it home. I shot her a reply and then put the phone down beside me and closed my eyes, not opening them again until I was pulled awake by another notification from my phone.

My immediate assumption had been that it was a response from Laurel, so I was surprised to Desiree's name there instead, with a text message instead of a call.

"He wants to see you tonight. Are you available?"

I pushed out a sigh. I'd just been with him the night before – vigorously enough that I'd woken up alone in the hotel room with sore nipples and sore thighs. Somehow… those seemed like reasons *to* see him again, instead of reasons *not* to.

And it wasn't like I had other plans, since surely dozing in front of the TV didn't count. I'd showered as soon as I got home from the center, so I was halfway ready to go anyway…

I picked up my phone, staring at the words in the text for just a few more moments before I tapped out a reply.

"Sure. What time?"

The darkness intensified everything.

I couldn't figure out who had the unfair advantage, me or him. But as I laid out across the bed, legs spread wide, panting as I tried to breathe normally again after yet *another* explosive orgasm, I definitely *felt* like I was getting the better end of this deal.

"Tell me how you came to be what you are today."

I startled at the words – first because I hadn't heard him come back into the room, then because he was speaking to me at all, and finally because of the content of the question. The two times before, there hadn't been any conversation, no pillow talk and cuddling after the deed was done. So for *that* to be the first thing out of his mouth... I really didn't know what to say.

"Excuse me?" I asked, seeking clarity as I sat up, blindly feeling for the covers to wrap around my naked frame. "I'm not sure what you're asking."

"The Cartwright Center," he came back. The bed shifted a bit under his weight as he sat down – another discrepancy from the "norm". "Program Director, Manager, whatever your title is... you run the place. How did that happen?"

Behind my mask, I tried to raise an eyebrow. "I'm pretty sure you've looked into me enough that you know the answer to that. Know everything about me."

"I know what the internet says about Rowan, but I don't know... *Rowan.* I'd like you to enlighten me."

I ran a hand through my hair, absently attempting to tame my sex-matted kinks. "I... didn't think that was part of the agreement."

"Does it have to be in the contract? I can't just want to talk to you?"

"It's not that you *can't*," I answered, shaking my head. "It's more that I just didn't think you wanted to. It's not the precedent that was set."

"A mistake I'll own," he said, from much closer than he'd been a moment before. I shivered at the touch of his hand on my bare thigh, held my breath as he moved it up, stopping at my hip.

86

"But, just so that you know…" his hand moved from my leg to my chin, shifting my head in a way that undoubtedly would've left me looking him in the eyes if it weren't for the mask. "Please don't mistake my enthusiasm for, and expertise at making you cum for disinterest in the other things I find attractive about you. You understand?"

I swallowed hard, slightly embarrassed by the way the cockiness in his words sent a tremble through me. "Yes. Duly noted."

"Thank you," he told me, in that resonant, sexy voice – the same voice he'd always had, only now, after three of these… "meetings"… it felt different. *Familiar.* "So now then… back to my question. How does a well-educated, ambitious, gorgeous woman end up running a struggling community center?"

I wanted to be a little offended by the "struggling" part, but considering that the "struggle" was the whole reason I was in this room in the first place, I swallowed that feeling.

"Loyalty, I guess." I raised my shoulders, and then dropped them again. "I've gotten other job offers, could've done something else. Maybe would've been more successful at something else. But the Cartwright Center is just… engrained in me, I guess. Growing up, it was a safe place to study, play with my friends, have a meal. I was always right beside Janie when she was still alive, running this place. I saw the impact it had then, and I still the impact now. I can't just give up on it."

"So you think that's the only way you make an impact? Couldn't you do something else? Something other than putting a band-aid over their needs… and knees?"

I frowned. "A band-aid over their needs?"

"Yeah." He'd already dropped his hand from my face, but he shifted closer, enough that I could feel the heat from his body.

"A lot of what the Cartwright Center does – the lunch program you want to do, for example – it's about filling in a gap, right?"

"Right."

"Okay, so what if, instead constantly having to provide the meals, the source got fixed. Better wages for the parents, better nutrition education, better public transportation for access to the stores..."

"Ah, so politics, huh?"

"Yeah."

"Uh, *no*," I laughed, without even feeling bad over killing the enthusiasm in his voice. "All that political stuff? Just sounds good to talk about, honestly. I have zero confidence in the government when it comes to making a real difference for people in need."

"Wow. So you... what, you just don't trust politicians?"

"Not even a little," I agreed. "And I feel bad for the new ones, running on these "hope" and "change" platforms. I know they mean well, but they're going to get in there and realize that nobody gives a shit except them. All those millionaire lawmakers care about is themselves, their millions, and their millionaire friends."

"Damn," he chuckled. "That's a pretty cynical position to take."

"It's a *realistic* position to take. I... you asked how I ended up running a "struggling" community center? Well, it wasn't always struggling. But then one politician after another, all of whom promised to make things better, and be there for the "people", and look out for children, the usual bullshit... little by little I've watched funding get stripped from vital programs. The programs that kept our children fed, kept our parks clean and safe, helped us be a resource. We've gone from thriving to barely afloat, all under the reign of politicians who promised it wouldn't be that way. So you have to forgive my… skepticism."

He pushed out a sigh, but didn't say anything for a few moments. "I understand. I'm sorry you're feeling let down. I still think our communities are better served by solving the roots of our problems, but that doesn't change the fact that people like you, places like the Cartwright Center, are necessary. Those kids *do* need you. There's no reason for you to not have what you need."

"There may not be a reason, but the reality is what it is," I countered. "I was supposed to have what I needed, but I didn't. So I took it into my own hands, and here we are… debauchery for money."

As soon as those words left my mouth, an air of tension fell over the room, making me shift uncomfortably in my spot on the bed.

"Debauchery?" he asked, his tongue forming the word so deliberately that I could tell he was surprised I'd used it.

I swallowed, clearly sensing that he was bothered. "I mean… what else would you call this? It's not legal, it's immoral, it's…"

"A mutually beneficial arrangement. You get something you need, and so do I."

I scoffed. "Yeah, but you're not being paid to degrade yourself."

"Degrade?" Nick laughed – a sound I didn't know I needed to hear until it was happening, warming me from head to toe. "Tell me," he said, leaning in to kiss my shoulder before he lowered his mouth to my ear. "When did you feel degraded? When I pulled you on top of my face so I could be fully immersed in the decadence of your pussy? When I had your toes in my mouth? When I—"

"*Stop*," I snapped, as my face grew hot.

"Why, Rowan? I'm trying to understand when exactly *I* did something to you in this room that made you feel *degraded*."

"I…" I shook my head, infuriated by the embarrassed tears forming in my eyes, and grateful for the mask to hide them. "You… haven't."

"You're goddamn right I haven't. I haven't done *shit* but revere you, so now I need to understand why that bullshit even came out of your mouth."

"Why wouldn't it?!" I exclaimed. "Are we about to pretend that having sex for money is some *normal* thing?!"

"This is Vegas, beautiful. A thousand transactions are happening as we speak."

I pulled the covers tighter around me. "But I'm… I'm *not* that girl."

"Bullshit," he argued. "You're *exactly* that girl – or are you a figment of my imagination, and you're not really here right now?"

"*Fuck you*. How dare you speak to me like this, like *you* aren't the one who approached me with this shit?!"

He chuckled again. "Yeah, I did. I saw you. I admired you. I wanted you, so I did what it took to get you. That go-getter attitude was something I thought we had in common, but apparently not, since you're *not that girl*."

"Excuse me?" I frowned.

"You're not hard of hearing, Rowan. I admired your determination – your willingness to do whatever the fuck you had to do to keep that center open. I get the gift of your presence for a month – *you* get perks that the Cartwright Center will be benefitting from for years and years to come, but you can sit in my face whining about "degrading yourself" like *every-fucking-body* doesn't have a price – most of them a lot goddamn lower

90

than yours. I have a lot more respect for a woman that uses whatever resources she has to better her position than one that sits back and lets the shit happen to her and then plays the victim."

Before I could think about it, before I could calculate the risk, before I could consider the consequences, my hand had swung out, blindly connecting with his face.

"*Fuck you*," I hissed, even though I'd said it already, and had no business further antagonizing him. Apparently though, I wasn't in control of my body – I certainly didn't *intend* to put my hands out, wildly, sightlessly grabbing in his direction. I made contact with his shirt, using it to pull myself toward him, and the next thing I knew I was climbing on top of him, lowering my face to his with startling aggression.

At first, my lips smashed against his forehead, but that was what I needed to get my bearings and properly aim for his lips. Any intentions I had of controlling that kiss were quickly overshadowed – as soon as our mouths connected, he consumed me.

He kept my mouth where he wanted by fisting handfuls of my hair as he kissed me, licked me, devoured me. My clumsy hands worked their way between our bodies, undoing his belt, unbuttoning and unzipping the pants I didn't understand why he'd put back on, freeing him from his boxers. I frantically worked my way into position and then sank down onto him, moaning as my body adjusted to accept him.

And then we both went still.

His grip on my hair softened, and we stayed there, face to face, him inside of me, saying nothing. We weren't kissing anymore, but we were still right there in each other's space, swapping air – him seeing everything, me seeing nothing.

I dipped my head, and then adjusted my hips, allowing him to settle deeper into me. Behind the mask, I closed my eyes – squeezed them tight – trying to hold back the inexplicable tears that were threatening to break free.

"I… I need to see your face," I said, not even knowing *why* that came out of my mouth. That was quickly becoming a theme for me, apparently – just doing things with no rhyme, reason, or explanation.

He brought his lips to mine, but didn't kiss me. "No you don't, beautiful. I'm nobody of consequence to you."

"That's not true. If it was true, you'd show me your face."

No response.

"Nick…I—*Ah!*"

Before I could make another appeal, he'd rocked his hips in an upward stroke that snatched the words from my lips. Then his hands were at my waist, holding me where he wanted me while he did it again, and again, and again, until I'd forgotten any questions or concerns I'd previously felt the need to state. Instead, I chose to focus on the euphoric feeling of having him inside of me, his hands gripping my ass, his mouth on my neck.

I focused on riding him.

Like this situation was something different than what it was. Like I *wanted* to be here, because I did. Like I wanted to cum, and make him cum, because I did, no matter how much I may not have wanted to admit it. Like I wanted him to leave this room thinking about my pussy, because I *did.*

Because if I was honest with myself… I wasn't thinking about the Cartwright Center when I came here tonight.

I was thinking about *his* dick.

Laurel wanted me to do something for *me,* and here it was.

I had *every* intention of enjoying it.

"I'll be contacting you directly, from now on," I said, placing a brand new smartphone on the dresser. It had already been through the ringer with Des' tech people, so I trusted it damn near better than I trusted my own personal one.

So I'd gotten one just like it, to contact her with.

"The number is already saved, so you'll know it's me."

From her perch on the bed, she nodded. "Okay. Is there an expectation that I'll always answer it immediately?"

"Of course not," I told her, grinning. "You're a grown woman. I'd like you to be responsive, obviously, but I don't expect you to be waiting by the phone either."

"Understood."

Shit.

I'd gotten her talking earlier and then fucked it up, pushing her too far. But it had gotten under my skin, hearing her speak down on herself. Especially with the shit that I knew went down around here – in Vegas in general, but even more so among the rich, and *especially* among rich politicians. If this all got aired out, people would treat it like some huge scandal for the sake of having something to talk about, but honestly?

It was just another Tuesday.

It was a little rich of me to feel so indignant about it, when I was the one who'd put her in this position. A better man – a less selfish one – would have seen her need and met it. But I... I'd just had to get something out of it.

And honestly speaking? Tonight had been more of what I wanted from her than the two nights before.

Her beauty was what got my attention. The fire in her spirit, the determination in her voice as she argued for that grant had been what kept it. Her quiet dignity – her refusal to allow her disappointment over losing it to show on her face, her immediate kindness to her opponent... that had solidified it.

I wanted to know more.

And everything I learned made me want *her* more.

She wasn't just talking shit about helping people, wasn't raising a ruckus just for show, like so many. She was *actually* about that action – evidenced by the contract she'd signed. Unconventional, sure, but she wasn't sitting around waiting to be saved – she made the best deal she possibly could.

I hated that she didn't see it that way.

I didn't say goodbye.

My attempt at making conversation had made things awkward enough between us. I'd pissed her off, sure, but I doubt she knew the effect *her* words had on me.

She'd spoken life to my worst nightmares.

I wasn't naïve, I didn't think. I knew that much of politics was occupied by bullshit and bullshitters, but I desperately wanted to *not* be part of that. I had lofty – maybe unrealistic – goals of being someone to actually get shit down, but the more I saw, the less faith I had.

I wasn't so sure anymore if it was worth it.

"Reid Bennett!" I heard, as soon as I – inadvertently – stepped off the elevator into the main lobby of the hotel. I was supposed to be meeting my security in the sub-lobby, outside the view of the general public, but I'd been so consumed with thoughts of Rowan that I wasn't thinking as clearly as I should.

Looking up, my eyes scanned until they landed on Jeff Perry, and I fought the urge to roll my eyes. Of *all* the people to run into at a hotel, this motherfucker was one of the last I wanted to see.

"Jeff, how are you?" I asked, putting on the same fake smile I kept ready for any public appearance, accepting his hand when he offered it.

Jeff shook his head. "Man, I am doing much better than you after those latest poll numbers I think. You're getting your ass kicked in this politics thing, man. You think maybe it's not really your thing?"

"I think that I am not about to get tricked into giving you a quote – like I suspect you did to the woman from the community center," I told him, looking him right in the eyes. "That article definitely took a shot, man."

He smirked. "My bad. You know I believe in you, Reid, but we have to report the truth."

"You keep up the good fight then, aiight?"

"Most definitely. What are you doing here man? It's a little late for any um… campaign meetings, right?"

I kept my expression impassive. "Work doesn't have a time frame. It ends when it ends. What are you doing here?"

"Staying here, until I get my new place set up. Drake properties are known for their, ah… discretion. A factor I'm sure you can appreciate."

Hmph.

Jeff was working hard to get a rise out of me, but I wasn't giving him the satisfaction.

"It's Vegas, Jeff. Everybody appreciates discretion. I'll see you around," I told him, turning to head towards the stairs that would take me where I needed to be. Everything was all good until he called after me.

"You'll be at the Armstrong Gala next weekend, right?"

I stopped to turn and answer him. "Yes, I will. But I already have a plus one, I'm afraid."

He laughed. "Yeah, I would think so. That gorgeous fiancée of yours. Enid Grant, right?"

"You already know that."

"I do," he nodded. "And I think you know my date as well…?"

I raised an eyebrow. "I do?"

"Yeah. That *fine ass* director from the Cartwright Center. Rowan Phillips."

I tamped down the hot, instant annoyance that filled my chest, again forcing myself to keep my true feelings off my face. Instead, I let my eyebrow go higher as I grinned. "*Really* now?" I asked, feigning respect. "That's quite a catch."

"You see it," Jeff joked, with a nod. "Anyway… we'll see you there. Have your checkbook ready for a donation to the center."

I nodded. "My checkbook stays ready, my man."

With that, I turned away, knowing I was barely keeping my anger in check. Rowan and I had been in that room for hours, she *knew* what our contract stipulations were, and she hadn't found it pertinent to mention *this* shit?

I bluff out a huff of air as I headed down the one flight of stairs.

I knew better than to act on anything Jeff said without getting the real story for myself, and besides that… I wasn't that concerned anyway.

I wasn't a man that buckled in the face of competition – my failing campaign was evidence of that. I wasn't going down without a fight.

I was just gonna work harder.

Seven.

"And I stand by my assertion that service work is more impactful than politics, at least in the current environment. Why waste time begging these crusty old men to do right when we can just do it ourselves? Is it hard? Of course! Do we need more money? OF COURSE! But honestly… is the other option even viable at this point? We can't even get these idiots to agree that there should be universal background checks to buy a gun! You REALLY think they give a damn if some Black kids only eat during the school tear? They don't!"

I finished typing out that text, hit send, and then couldn't help the smile that spread across my face. Since late morning, I'd been going back and forth with a man whose name *definitely* wasn't Nick, but was saved as such in the phone he'd given me several days ago.

The last time I'd "seen" him.

But even without physically being in the same space, he'd certainly made his presence known.

I'd forgotten the butterfly-inducing feeling of texting back and forth all day, specifically with a man who had much more to say than "wyd", or "gm". No, "Nick" was all, "What's on your agenda today", and "make sure you stop to eat, you have to take care of yourself", and "what are your thoughts on the mess this administration is making of immigration". There were no… lulls. No nagging feeling of *"I wish this man would leave me alone"*, more like, *"I love that he doesn't take forever to hit me back"*, even though there was no doubt in my mind that he was a busy man.

Politics was a steadily moving, growing beast.

He was smart enough to know that his obvious passion about the subject was a clue for me, but one that must not have mattered, since he hadn't backed off or tried to cover his tracks. To my own personal credit, I tamped down the urge to try to look into it, and talked Laurel out of it too. It was information I couldn't do anything with, and crazy enough... I felt safer *not* knowing. Besides that, with the current environment, I ignored politics as much as I could anyway, so I barely knew who the players were – something I intended to keep that way.

What if Nick was a conservative?

Just the thought made me shudder.

"You're making it very hard for me to hold on to my ideals, Ms. Phillips. Your gift of persuasion is both admirable and loathsome. Your words tap right into my desire to work directly with the people I want to help, but I have to tamp that passion down to be effective in my current position. – Nick."

"You don't expect me to apologize for that, do you?"

"Absolutely not. I would be disappointed if you did, because as difficult as it is, I appreciate the challenge you've placed in front of me. – Nick."

"Challenge? Is that how you view me now? Why you've not wanted to see me?"

"Have you lost your mind? – Nick."

"There hasn't been a moment since the last time I saw, touched, smelled, tasted you, that I haven't wanted to return to our rendezvous. I've been insanely busy, and... tending to my other obligations. – Nick."

Hmph.

Through our conversations over the last few days, I knew that "other obligations" meant keeping his ass at his – probably marital – home. I didn't remember seeing a tan line or indentation on his finger that first night, when I'd seen his hands, but what other reason would a grown ass man have to be confined at home?

Sleeping with a married man had always been a hard line I refused to cross. Contributing to another woman's pain was a deal breaker for me.

I thought.

I had nothing other than my own suspicions telling me that "Nick" was probably not as single as he and Desiree Byers claimed, but those suspicions rarely led me wrong. Still, hearing him speak out his "familial obligations" to his "current position" also had me suspicious that whatever *public* relationship he was in, wasn't much different than the one between he and I.

A business transaction.

Did that make it right? *Of course not.* But I was already so wrong that I doubted it made much difference.

"I can guarantee that I am, in fact, in possession of my mind. It was just a question."

"With an answer I thought I'd made more than obvious. My desire for you has not wavered, Rowan. Only grown. – Nick."

With a sigh, I pushed the phone away without replying to that, because it was the type of thing that would get me in trouble. The more we talked, the more he made such statements, the harder it was for me to tell myself that this was just sex, and that it would all be over in a few weeks.

What more than sex could it be anyway, Rowan? You've never even seen his face!

I held on to that self-admonition as I returned the phone to my desk drawer, intent on getting some work done. As good as I was at multi-tasking, it was a little difficult to design preschool curriculum when you were busy… flirting. Or whatever Nick and I had been doing.

When I heard a familiar buzz from the drawer, I sighed, knowing that Nick was probably wondering why I hadn't texted back. I worked for ten more minutes and then pulled the drawer open, eyes widening in surprise when I realized that it was my *other* phone with the notification.

It was a text from Jeff Perry.

Not that I had his number saved in my phone, but he'd included it in the body of a text inquiring after my answer to his invitation to the gala that was fast-approaching.

Shit.

Neither Jeff nor the gala had even been on my mind, now that Nick was... I don't know what Nick was doing, but I liked it, whatever it was.

That didn't change the fact that I'd left Jeff hanging so far, and hadn't even done what I was supposed to do as far as finding out if it was okay for me to go. It was a *great* networking opportunity, so I wasn't really keen to miss it, but with the way Nick had been occupying my consciousness for the last few days... I wasn't sure about asking to go anywhere on Jeff's arm.

So what, is he your boyfriend now?

That thought was just the little holt I needed to shake my head, brushing off whatever unsuitable, untimely feelings had me feeling loyal to Nick. It was, like I'd said, just a business transaction – when this was over, he'd have a different woman sign a contract to his bed.

I texted Jeff back that I would have an answer for him tomorrow and then shut the phone completely off, intent on finishing up my work. But no sooner than I'd really found my focus and dived in, another notification buzzed.

"I thought I turned this damn thing off," I wondered out loud as I pulled the drawer open again. I quickly realized that this time, it *was* from the phone Nick had given me, which was still powered on. Very, *very* briefly, I entertained turning *it* off too, without even looking at the text. I'd forgotten that any man who brought butterflies usually brought drama too. *That* was the part I hadn't missed.

Still, I couldn't bring myself to not even look, and once I did, I was glad that I had.

"Have lunch with me? – Nick."

He'd never requested my presence during the day, always preferring to conduct our business when it was dark outside. I knew he wasn't talking about sitting down somewhere in public, but maybe...

"I can't eat lunch wearing a mask ☺*."*

"I'll feed you. – Nick."

I sighed.

As sexy as I may have found such an offer in any other context, I was really, *really* tired of the mask. Sure, I'd agreed to it, and *sure*, it made the sex hotter, but beyond that, I was over it. I didn't even care who he was, not really. I didn't need a real name.

I just wanted to see his face.

But I already knew the answer to *that.*

"What time?"

"Now. The car is two minutes away from you. I was hoping you'd say yes. – Nick."

More like assuming, I quietly fumed. I packed my things away to come back to afterward – if he didn't decide to keep me in the room all night – and then grabbed both phones, slipping them into my purse. I didn't bother stopping by a mirror to check myself – if he wanted me in the middle of the day, he got whatever he got.

I didn't stay pissed long.

Couldn't stay pissed long.

Not once I smelled his cologne, and felt his hands, not once I melted into the panty-dissipating hug and kiss combo he used to greet me.

"Open up."

After hearing that from him in a much more demanding tone, in a much different context than he meant it now, those two little words made me blush, but I did I was told. I opened my mouth, letting him insert a fork loaded with the most amazing salad greens I'd ever tasted, tossed in the most amazing vinaigrette I'd ever tasted. The rest of the meal had gotten a similar descriptor.

"Another one of those shrimp next, please," I asked, making him laugh.

"Another? You're still working on the first one – I cut it in pieces."

"Okay whatever, just give it."

"Okay, damn," he chuckled again. "I gotcha skrimps coming, woman."

When I was finished chewing, I giggled. "Skrimps? Not a phrasing I expected to come out of *your* mouth, even in humor."

"I didn't always talk like I was giving a speech, Rowan. *Don't* always."

I nodded. "Yeah, I've caught your little slips here and there. Assumed you were probably…"

"A converted hood nigga? Guilty as charged."

I almost knocked over my water aiming for it in the darkness behind my mask as I giggled. "Not how I would have

102

verbalized it, but… yes. So how did you end up here from there? Bootstraps?"

Please don't say bootstraps…

"*Hell* no," he declared, and I knew he was shaking his head, even though I couldn't see it. "Yes, I was in the hood, just a few wards over, actually. Banged a lil bit, never got caught or nothing, but one of the old heads knew I had a good head on my shoulders – stayed on me about my grades, contrary to popular belief about… everything hood related. He wanted me out of there. On something better. When I was maybe seventeen, a Black politician came to talk to the school. Got the rims stolen off his car actually," Nick laughed. "But he talked to us about registering to vote when we turned eighteen, being a part of the political process and all that. About how it could make a real difference. I bought *right* into that shit."

"He was crooked, wasn't he?"

"As the fucking Grand Canyon," he chuckled. "But like I said, I bought into it. Helped organize rallies, helped with voter registration, all that. And this was pre-Obama, so there weren't a lot of *us* who really thought it would make a difference, but I tried. The politician saw it too, valued it. Mentored me, wrote my college recommendations, all of that. He's done a lot for me. I… owe him a lot."

Something about his inflection there made me frown. "Owing" a crooked politician wasn't exactly an enviable position, but I brushed it off, focusing on the other parts of the story.

"So that explains how you got into politics, but not how you got money. Money to blow on struggling community centers and sex contracts," I teased.

"Tech," he answered. "I double-majored. Computer Science and Political Science. I wanted to build something related to political stats, poll numbers, and all of that, but I worried about it being a conflict of interest somehow when I wanted to enter the ring myself later. So, instead… and this is top secret information, Rowan. You can't tell anybody this, and couldn't prove it either way, but… very quietly, there's an app that sports organizations use. College, professional, even internationally. It automatically gathers data from the internet – stats about every game, every player, and delivers a forecast. How many points they'll average, how likely they are to have an injury, how many years they'll last in the game. They use it to figure out what they'll pay, who they'll draft, how many years to contract for, all that."

I frowned. "Oh bullshit. That doesn't even sound legal for real use."

"Legal or not, I don't know or care. The fact is, I made it, it works scarily well, and I got *paid*. Majorly paid. And my name is nowhere near it anymore – scrubbed off of everything, so if they get sued, it's not my damn problem."

"Smart man," I nodded. "Because that sounds like a major lawsuit waiting to happen. But… it's a brilliant idea. The kind of brilliance your community could use, rather than it wasting away at the statehouse, or Congress, or wherever you're from."

He laughed. "That was a smooth segue."

"Well, I do try. Can I have another skrimp now?"

"You can have anything you want from me."

My eyebrows bunched as they lifted automatically behind the mask, impeded by the fabric. "Don't say that. Not while I'm wearing this thing."

"You're right. My apologies. *Almost* anything."

I smiled. "Another bite of the shrimp will suffice."

We spent the rest of the meal in relative silence. I only knew he was eating too because of the clinks of the fork against

104

the plate that weren't followed by a gentle demand for me to open my mouth. When the meal was over, I expected to be taken to the bed, but instead, he left me at the table for a moment before he came back, placing a small, velvet box in my hands.

He didn't say anything until he was behind me, his strong hands resting on my shoulders. "I have to leave, but, I want to see your reaction to this before I do. Don't look back at me, but… you can pull your mask up to see what's in the box."

I turned toward him, with the mask still covering my eyes. "Do you really trust me not to look?"

"I do. You're one of the most honest, principled people I know. And I know a *lot* of people. I absolutely believe you'll honor my wish for you to not see my face."

Damnit.

I hated that he was so right – there was no way I'd dishonor our contract to catch a glimpse without his consent, because if it were the other way around, I'd want my wishes honored as well. That didn't mean I had to like it though.

I turned back around, moving the box between my fingers for a moment before I raised a hand, using it to pull the mask up over my eyes. Once it was secure against my forehead, I opened the box, and immediately gasped.

In the box was a pair of *gorgeous* sapphire earrings, each one made up of two pear-shaped sapphires, dangling from opposing ends and surrounded by diamonds. The necklace was simpler – just one sapphire, but still surrounded by diamonds, hanging from a delicate platinum chain.

"Nick," I breathed, not taking my eyes away from the jewelry, which had to cost more than a year of my rent. Maybe five years of my rent. "I *can't* accept this."

"You can," he replied, leaning to speak the words into my ear before he pressed a kiss to my temple. "You will. And it'll be beautiful on you."

I shook my head. "I don't even have anywhere to... I... actually, um... there was something I was supposed to ask you, that seems completely inappropriate to ask now, so... nevermind."

"No," he insisted, raising to a stand again. "Ask."

Pushing out a deep sigh, I let the words rush out. "Jeff Perry asked me to accompany him to the Armstrong Gala. It's not a date – not to me. It's a networking opportunity that I need, and I—"

"*Go.*"

I stopped speaking, paralyzed by that one word. "I'm sorry?"

"You heard me, Rowan. I think you should go. Like you said... it's a networking opportunity that you shouldn't miss. As long as Mr. Perry understands that while you're welcome to be on his arm for the night, he is *not* welcome—"

"In me," I finished for him. "There won't be any concern about that, no matter *what* Mr. Perry thinks. For two and a half more weeks... I'm yours, and yours only."

There was a lengthy pause where I expected him to agree, or something. But when he *did* speak, it wasn't with conviction, it was with... disappointment.

"Yes. For two and a half more weeks."

After that, there was another length of silence, one where I stared at Nick's generous gift and regretted even bringing Jeff's invitation up.

"Put your mask back on, Rowan," Nick said, breaking the silence with a request that caught me off guard.

"Really? I thought you were leaving?"

106

"I was," he said, pulling the mask down for me since I hadn't moved. He pulled the box from my hands, putting it God knows where before he pulled me up from my chair and easily lifted me to the table.

"And now?" I asked, pushing myself up to aid him in the removal of my panties from underneath my simple tee shirt dress.

I heard the chair move, and then felt his breath on my thighs as he positioned himself between them.

"Now, I've remembered I couldn't leave lunch until I'd devoured the last course."

"That must've been *some* lunch."

I pushed out a hard breath, trying to convince myself not to put Enid out of my house, simply because she'd spoken to me. Our dynamic hadn't been healthy for a long, *long* time. Now? The shit was flat-out toxic.

And exactly what I *didn't* need right now.

Lunch with Rowan had been great. Good food, good conversation, with a woman I couldn't get enough of. I knew about the gala thing already of course, had even had the jewelry purchased for her with that in mind. But it *still* stung to hear her ask about going out with goddamn *Jeff.*

Fuck Jeff.

His nosy ass was the reason I hadn't seen her in days – trying to lay low, avoid being seen again at the Drake. I'd only been seen, period, because of my own negligence that day, but the damage was done now. If he saw me there again, he'd know there was a story. Not *what* story, just *a* story, and once that was the case, there was no coming back from it.

I just couldn't stay away.

But this time, I did it the right way – private elevator, we'd changed rooms, changed cars, everything. And honestly? It was less about *me* being found out than it was about Rowan. I didn't want her caught in the crossfires of anything.

What I *wanted* was to have her pack a bag, I'd pack one too, and we'd just run away.

But I knew that couldn't happen.

Not with the position I was in, not now.

Instead of saying anything to Enid, I finished the removal of my jacket and threw it across the couch in my office, doing my best to ignore her.

"You were gone for *three* hours," she continued, from right behind me. When I turned, she stepped even closer to me, completely invading my personal space. "And you came back *smelling like her.* Your ass is so disrespectful."

"Get the fuck out of my office before I do something we *both* regret," I warned, only to have it met with a smirk.

"Like *what*, Reid? We both know you aren't gonna do shit – me and Daddy stripped all the "hood" out of you. Remember?"

I scoffed. "The "hood" doesn't have a goddamn thing to do with it."

"Doesn't it though?" Enid sneered. "You *reek* of the exact kind of sixty-dollar perfume some bitch from your past probably thinks is high-end. Hell, *you* probably think it's high end. Did you buy it for her?"

"What the hell do you want?"

"Do I have to *want* something to talk to my fiancée? You've been spending so much more time at home, I thought you were finally coming back to me. But then… you don't even wash her off of you before you come home. Interesting."

"Interesting?"

"Yes, interesting. I know she's not the *first* of your whores, but... she must be *special.*"

I chuckled. "I don't have "whores", Enid – unless you're referring to yourself. And even then, you're the only one deserving of that title. But go ahead - convince yourself that you and I are the same, if that's what it takes to live with yourself."

"Oh we are *absolutely* the same, my love," Enid smirked. "You're in this for the politics as much as I am, you just still, for some reason, think you're noble. You're *naïve.* That's why you're so mad at me Reid, so disgusted. Because I played this game better than you – I *actually* got your simple ass to fall in love."

"Enid..."

"What is that, another warning?" she went on, laughing. "Again – you're not gonna do anything. Your proximity to my family is too important to you – you *know* my father would destroy you if there was even a *whiff* of you hurting me. And because you're a fucking coward, that's enough to keep you right in line."

"*Is it though?*" I asked, rounding on her, stepping into *her* face. "I've just about decided to say fuck this campaign, fuck politics period, so you really may not want to play with me. This is real life, not a game like it is for you. So don't be surprised when the moves *I* make are a little more fucking brutal than yours."

I was relieved to see real fear in Enid's eyes – hoped it was enough for her to drop this conversation, but I knew her a little too well for that. Knew she didn't like to lose.

She shuttered the fear in her eyes, narrowing them in defiance instead. "Am I supposed to be afraid you're gonna put your hands on me? Let me put this in terms you can understand a little better – *you ain't that nigga*, Reid Bennet for City Council. At least not since we got our hands on you."

"Oh no I've never been *that* nigga," I corrected, moving even closer, forcing her to step back. "I don't beat up women, never felt a need to. So when I threaten to *do* something, please rest assured that physical harm isn't what I have on my mind. I'm talking about the type of shit that stains the public perception forever. But if Kim Kardashian flipped it into a career, I'm certain you can too."

Her eyebrows lifted in understanding. "You're threatening me with revenge porn?! Are you kidding?! What happened to all your values?"

"My values are perfectly intact, *my love*," I sneered. "I, personally, would never release imagery of you in any compromising position, but ol' boy that you were screwing around with behind my back? He has no such qualms."

Enid's nostrils flared in anger. "What are you saying?"

"I'm saying, that it would a shame if you didn't get the fuck outta my face and I decided to stop paying him to keep your whole pussy off the internet. Oh, damn – you didn't know we had that deal, did you? And you've still been seeing him, haven't you? Wow, gorgeous. That's really messed up."

She shoved away from me, wiping away sudden tears. "You're a fucking monster, you know that?"

I moved to go to my desk, which had been my original destination before she decided to poke at me, and gotten more of a reaction that she anticipated.

"Maybe so," I shrugged, unmoved by her obviously hurt feelings. "But if I am… guess who created me?"

Eight.

"I'm sorry, is that American dollars?!"

Laurel laughed at my reaction to the - in my broke ass opinion - exorbitant price tag attached to the deep blue dress she'd insisted I try on without looking at the price first - a mistake, because now my damn feelings were hurt.

This was *the* dress.

I slid my hands down my hips, admiring the way the luxurious fabric draped over my curves, catching and beautifully reflecting the light every time I moved. Off-shoulder sleeves, a sweetheart neckline, a fit that molded softy over my hips before the skirt flared into sweeping layers, complete with a short train. My *everything* looked great in that dress, and God knows I didn't want to take it off, but...

"Ro, you really act as if your financial situation hasn't drastically changed. Are you not collecting an actual salary at the center now?"

I sighed. "I know, but still. The quickest way to go back to being broke is to start spending money willy-nilly. You've seen what happens to most lottery winners, right?"

"Is that how it feels?" Laurel teased, stepping beside me to admire my reflection with me. "Like you hit the jackpot?"

"More like some weird Cinderella-Rumpelstiltskin mash-up," I mused.

She laughed. "So does that mean you think Jeff is your Prince Charming?"

"God no," I huffed. "I mean, don't get me wrong, Jeff is handsome, and charming, and all that, but he's..."

"Not Mr. Fifty Shades of Nigga?"

"Bye."

Laurel and I laughed at the same time, just as another small group entered the fitting area, accompanied by the salesperson we'd told we didn't need any assistance. The newcomers obviously had no such self-sufficiency – the saleslady looked nervous as hell as she showed the group of four, headed by Enid Grant, into the showroom

There was my sign, right there, that I had no business here.

I didn't have an Enid Grant sort of budget.

Well… I *didn't,* in the two minutes before she walked into the place like she owned it, stopped her vapid, giggly conversation with her friends to look me over and then turn to the saleslady and point.

"I want to try that on for the gala."

Every woman in the room immediately clocked how ridiculous that was, because the room went silent, until the saleslady stammered, "Um… well, Ms. Grant, we don't carry multiples… all of our pieces are one of a kind."

"Duh," Enid rudely drawled, looking to her minions for support. "I want you to take that one off her. Now. I want to try that one first. Blue is my fiancé's favorite color."

"I'm not done with it yet," I spoke up, refusing to be bullied into falling in line with what she wanted, as she was probably used to most people doing. She probably didn't even remember me from that one year of high school, but I remembered her *well.*

I'd never taken kindly to that "mean girl" bullshit.

Enid snorted. "Oh *please.* With those nails and that hair… no way you can afford a piece like that. Now, it's time to move along and let the big girls with the real money play dress up. You and your little friend can have a glass of top shelf on me though.

Get them what they want," she said, turning to the saleslady again. "But not until after she's out of that dress."

"I said I wasn't done," I snapped, propping a hand on my hip. "And as a matter of fact… I'll take it," I told the flushed-looking sales clerk. "And *they* can have a glass on *me*. Well drinks though, cause I'll be a little light on cash after I pay for this dress." Smirking, I looked Enid right in her face, unmoved by an expression that probably struck fear in plenty of others. "Guess you'll have to a find a different *something blue* for your fiancé."

Enid's eyes narrowed. "Who the fuck are you?"

"Nobody," I shot back, turning back to my reflection, effectively dismissing her to smirk at Laurel in the mirror as she moved to help me take off the dress that I was, apparently, buying.

Making a point to Enid aside, the dress was, honestly, perfection. And it was just my luck that the gift of sapphires I'd gotten from my mystery man would be just the right additions to complete the look.

I was set… almost.

"Come on girl, let's go see what Target has in their shoe section," I told Laurel, as I slipped into the little robe I'd worn between dresses to cover my undergarments. She and I shared a laugh over the obvious disgust of Enid and her friends that I would openly admit to buying non-designer shoes, then moved on, taking the saleslady with us, since she'd technically assisted *us* first anyway.

Checkmate, bitch.

Why did I feel so aggressively pleased with myself for poking at Enid? I was too damn old to be holding on to high school stuff – especially when she'd never come directly at me – but it annoyed me that instead of leaving that behind and

113

becoming a better person, it appeared that she was still the same bully.

I hadn't taken it then, and I wasn't about to start now.

I took that adrenaline with me right to the register, where I depleted a large chunk of the savings I'd *finally* started building to pay for that dress. And then, I took my broke ass right down to Target, finding a pair of simple, elegant heeled sandals that were much more within my budget. And I didn't feel bad about it either – not only because I bought shoes there all the time anyway, when I had the money for it, because they were friggin' cute – but because all the attention would be on the dress and jewelry anyway.

I was going to look damn good.

If Jeff's reaction was any indication, I looked better – *much* better – than "damn good." His eyes nearly bulged out of his head when he arrived to pick me up, earning a teasing smirk and a few comments from Laurel that made me silently scold her. I'd agreed to have her see me off – and needed her help to get ready, honestly – but the last thing I needed was Jeff having it in his head that he was getting to see what was under this dress after the gala, like we were high-schoolers headed off to prom.

My lack of encouragement didn't keep his hands off the small of my back as he helped me out of the town car though.

Somehow, I didn't mind – I *needed* the extra fortification to not feel light-headed in a room full of Vegas elites. I wasn't typically intimidated by wealth – I'd put pride to the side to ask many of these people for donations to the center – but on this scale, it was... different.

114

Calling someone's office and getting rejected by their assistant was different than quite literally rubbing elbows with people who could fund the center for a year without even blinking about it. Familiar faces from the softball game stopped me to say hello, to say they loved what I was doing and planned to put checks in the mail. Nashira Drake stopped me to tell me I looked amazing. And not that it was the point of me coming out tonight, but *holy shit, Nashira Drake, of **the** Drakes thought I looked amazing!*

And again... so did Jeff.

"Ms. Phillips," he said, pulling me off to a quiet spot at the party, in a quest to get me to himself – something that hadn't happened since we walked in. There had been so many introductions – him keeping the networking promise he'd made, honestly – that we hadn't found ourselves alone at all in that first hour. Now, he was very into my personal space, smelling and looking good, but still not exactly sparking any heat in me.

Maybe because another man already has you ablaze...

"If I'd known you were going to show out like this, I would've thrown on something better than this," he teased, taking a step back to look me over again as I blushed.

"Oh please, you know you look like you came straight from a GQ shoot to accompany me, don't play."

Jeff grinned as he straightened his lapels. "This old thing? Nah, I should've come harder, matched your energy." He stepped in again, hand at my hip with a *very* friendly grip as he dipped his head. "You are wearing the *hell* outta this dress. All eyes on you, because you're the baddest thing in this room, and everybody knows it."

Skepticism colored the smile I gave him in response to those words, until I actually took a look around. There *were* quite a few eyes on me – cameras turned in my direction, long, appreciative glances from men and women, some glares from whoever they had on their arm. It wasn't *everyone*, not by a long shot, but enough to take note of. But there was one set of eyes in particular that sent a chill up my spine.

Enid.

She was openly scowling at me, paying no attention to what the man next to her was saying. The man? Former Congressman Julius Grant, who was currently in the running for a different seat, in a different district, after losing the one he'd previously held to a younger, more exciting candidate.

Probably the same miracle his soon-to-be son-in-law had hoped to perform against Doctor Betty Wheeler. Only, Reid's campaign was as good as over – as Mila had explained to me weeks ago, his district just wasn't ready to be headed by a young Black man.

Julius Grant's campaign, however, seemed to be going well.

That didn't make his daughter any more interested though.

She was *much* more invested in giving me the stink-eye.

Which was why I should've been much more alarmed when her glare suddenly turned into a smile as she headed for me, a luridly yellow cocktail in one hand, and a tiny plate of some kind of creamy hors-d'oeuvre in the other.

Maybe because I was an actual factual adult, it never occurred to me that she would "trip" as she approached, spilling the drink and plate all over the front of my dress and then making a huge spectacle of how sorry she was, to garner more attention. I took a step back, shocked by the intense cold of the drink – and the ice down my dress – so taken off guard that I actually stumbled out of my shoes and would have fallen if it weren't for

116

strong arms suddenly around my waist, steadying me until the ground was solid under my feet.

I looked back, expecting it to be Jeff, but he was a foot away, trying to calm Enid's hysterics as a crowd gathered around us.

My savior was Reid Bennett.

Looking like *hallelujah* in a beautifully tailored gray suit, with sapphire accents.

He smiled, but said nothing as he took a step back, grabbing my cheap target heels as cameras went off around us. I hadn't been embarrassed about them before, but I was *now*, now that *Reid Bennett for City Council* was kneeling in front of me, offering my shoes for me to slip my feet back into.

"Thank you," I stammered, using his offered shoulder as a balance to quickly get my shoes on, and out of sight. He gave me a long, lingering once-over that made heat rise to my cheeks. And then a nod, a smile, and then went to tend to his fiancée, relieving Jeff to come back to me.

"Damn," he grimaced, looking at my ruined dress. "Are you good?"

I scoffed. "Now that you're done checking on *her*… yeah, sure. I'm great."

I turned away from him to find Nashira Drake approaching me again, with a handful of napkins.

"Let's get you cleaned up," she insisted, and I followed, because this was technically a Drake party anyway, and if anyone could fix this, of course she could.

And of course she did.

Ten minutes, a google search, some club soda, several napkins and a blow dryer later, I was back out on the gala floor, looking just as good as I'd arrived. Jeff found me quickly, offering a glass of champagne and an apology that I accepted –

117

the champagne more than the apology. After that, he started going *extra* hard promoting the center, which started to grate on my nerves.

Or maybe it was just him.

I *wanted* to ask why the hell he'd been so concerned with helping her instead of me, but I knew it was just pride talking. I didn't honestly care, because I didn't honestly want Jeff.

There was only one man's attention I cared to have at this party, and I couldn't have it, assuming he was even here.

Rowan, you are officially crazy.

"Hey, come here," Jeff said, cupping my elbow to lead me to yet another potential donor. I almost stopped cold when I realized he was leading me to the Grants, who now had Reid in tow, the trio looking like every bit of Black Vegas royalty they were.

"Rowan," Enid said, through half-gritted teeth. "I see you got cleaned up. Aren't you resourceful?" she asked, in a tone that made it crystal clear she wasn't happy about it.

I smiled at her, then spoke loud enough to be heard over the chatter and loud music. "And I see you've learned my name."

She sneered. "Yes, well… it seems you have some sort of personal acquaintance with my fiancée."

"Do I?" I asked, eyebrows raised. "And what might that be?" I asked, looking directly at Reid.

He opened his mouth to speak, but was interrupted by Julius' commanding baritone cutting in – I didn't miss the flash of agitation in Reid's eyes, but he let the older man speak.

"It seems young Reid was a little overzealous in his community outreach – took over an event you were having for your softball team," Julius said, in what I could only assume was his campaign voice.

118

I forced a smile, and corrected, "Community center. The Cartwright Center. The softball game is just a thing we do during the summer – nowhere near the totality of who we are to that community."

"Oh, of course," he soothed, though I could tell he didn't really like my correction. "And you'll have to excuse my daughter for that little mishap earlier, with the drink. I don't know when she became a klutz – thought the finishing lessons would have taken care of that."

"Oh no worries," I said, waving him off. "I look good as new, so really… no harm, no foul. In fact… I heard a little rumor that blue was Reid's favorite color, and I see that he's wearing it tonight, as am I," – I stopped there, making it a point to look at Enid's champagne toned dress, that honestly clashed with his accents – "so I'll tell you what – if Reid will do me the honor of a dance, we'll consider all forgiven."

"Well I think that's a fair trade," Julius said, as I grinned right in Enid's face.

I turned from her to Reid, eyebrow raised, surprised to find a smirk on his handsome face. I didn't even have to ask if it was okay with him – he extended a hand, saying what I interpreted as "*shall we?*", even though I couldn't really hear over the fundraising announcement that came over the mic.

I accepted his hand with a nod, letting him lead me to the dance floor as the announcement wrapped up, and Enid's angry glare burned a hole in my bare back. I tried – and miserably failed – not to shudder at the electric feeling of Reid's bare skin on mine. Tried to talk myself out of feeling a little light-headed as the music started again, and Reid's hands went to my waist, pulling me close.

A little closer than he probably should, with a fiancé.

But I didn't care.

The way my heart was racing felt too familiar to.

"You look beautiful tonight," he practically yelled to be heard, instead of getting into my ear, which would have been even more inappropriate. But even with the distance, even with the innocent words, spoken loud enough for anyone to hear... it brought heat to my face.

And... another place.

Because he'd agitated me before, I'd only barely paid any real attention to how handsome Reid was. In honesty, the man was a walking wet dream – broad shoulders, deep chocolate skin, a square jaw and a beautiful smile. The kind of man that made your pulse quicken just because he walked into a room.

"Thank you," I managed to tell him, just before he pulled me closer as the crowd on the dance floor grew a little thicker. We were surrounded by couples doing the same standard slow-jazz two-step that we were, so I hoped we didn't particularly stand out.

Hoped we didn't *look* as hot as I *felt.*

Hoped he didn't hear what was happening in my head, which was... a lot.

And none of it was appropriate.

Because his touch was familiar, even though that was ridiculous. And his cologne was as soothing to my nose as walking into my apartment after a long day. And his arms... they felt like... *home.*

Which was crazy... right?

"*I knew those sapphires would look beautiful on you, Rowan,*" Reid murmured into my ear, his lips brushing my skin before he pulled back to an appropriate distance between our bodies and met my eyes, daring me to not put together the puzzle.

I stopped moving entirely, and my knees went a little weak, prompting him to tighten his arms around my waist, like he

120

had so many other times in that hotel room when we were alone, with me – *just me* – in the dark.

Those feelings weren't so crazy after all.

"Let me go," I hissed at him, suddenly finding it hard to breathe. When he didn't, I looked him right in the face, nostrils flared. "*Let me go, or I swear to God I will start screaming.*"

That seemed to do the trick, and I stormed off, gripping my tiny clutch so hard that I felt the plastic container of gum I had inside it pop open, but I didn't care. I just… I had to get away. I had to get somewhere, anywhere, but away from *here*.

"Rowan!" I heard, but didn't stop or turn back until I felt a hand on my arm. I turned in that direction, half-expecting to curse Reid out, but in a mirror from earlier, when Reid had rescued me… it was Jeff.

"Hey, what's going on?" he asked, getting in front of me. I'd completely forgotten about him, and honestly didn't want to be bothered with him now, but he was my ride.

Shit.

"Um… I just realized, I think I left the deep freezer open at the center when I left earlier," I lied, so smoothly that I scared myself a little. "That was hours ago, and it's probably working too hard to keep cold, and overloading the electrical system that doesn't get replaced until next month, and it's just… a disaster. If I left it open."

His eyes widened. "Well, come on. I can call the car, we'll go check it out."

"No," I shook my head. "No, you shouldn't have to leave for that. I'm just… I'm gonna step out, and call Mila. See if she remembers closing it, or if she can check it out for me. Just… go back to the party, and have fun. I'll find you once I get this cleared up. Just give me a second, okay?" I asked, and he nodded, seeming to buy it as I pulled my cell from my bag and stepped around the area that was obviously roped off to keep partygoers out. Once I'd found relative privacy in what appeared to be an empty meeting room, I took one more step, going out onto the private balcony to gulp in mouthfuls of the cool night air.

Reid Bennet.

Reid N. Bennet.

Reid Nicholas Bennet.

Nick.

"Rowan."

I nearly jumped out of my skin at the sound of *his* voice behind me. I turned to find him stepping out onto the balcony, all tall and fine and concerned and... *engaged.*

"You lied to me," came bursting from my lips as he reached for me, and I pushed his hands away.

He shook his head. "I did no such thing."

"I told you, told Desiree, that I wouldn't sleep with a married man!"

"And you *haven't.*"

"That's a goddamn technicality and you know it!" I snapped, then covered my mouth, remembering we were outside. "You are engaged. To *Enid Grant* of all people."

He scoffed. "What does that mean?"

"She is *disgusting*, Reid. And the fact that you're marrying her tells me everything I need to know about you."

"It doesn't tell you *shit*. Except maybe the fact that you and I have something in common – a willingness to make an undesirable choice for the greater good. Only difference... you're actually accomplishing that. Me? I've been stuck in this shit with nothing real to show for it."

"Oh don't you give me that bullshit," I groaned, shaking my head. "You're a grown ass man, Reid. Nobody can make you do anything you don't want."

122

He nodded. "You're absolutely right – which is why I'm suspending my campaign tomorrow. *Ending* my campaign. I'm telling Julius tonight, after the gala."

I rolled my eyes. "I don't believe a word out of your mouth."

"Then believe my actions, Rowan. Why the hell would I reveal myself to you here, tonight, if I wasn't about to do something drastic?" He stepped forward, grabbing my hand to lace his fingers through mine. "I... okay. Honestly, it wasn't supposed to be... *here*. But it was going to be tonight, after I told Julius, and broke it off with Enid. But then I saw you tonight, and you... you're so goddamn *beautiful*," he said, with this aching sort of reverence, as he looked me right in the eyes – something I'd been yearning before... before I knew it was him.

And now that I knew this is was him, that my mystery man was Reid Bennet... I couldn't look away. Couldn't pull away when he drew me closer, wrapping an arm around me as he backed us further into the shadows.

"I'm sorry to ruin your night, but I couldn't stand it another minute, especially after what Enid did to you."

I scoffed. "And what do you think she and her father would do to me now, if she knew... what we've been up to?"

"She doesn't know. And she won't. As far as she has to know, her antics tonight were what brought us together... since it's technically true."

I pushed out a sigh as I replayed it in my head, from the shock of the cold drink down my dress, to Reid kneeling to help me return my shoes to my feet at the ball... like my own personal Prince Charming.

So Laurel was halfway right... she just named the wrong Prince.

"This is too much," I told him, shaking my head as I back away, against the ivy-covered wall behind me. "The fact is that you're engaged to a beast of a woman, and have tight political ties with her father. I don't even know if I *like* Reid Bennet."

"After all the conversations we've had, can you *really* say that?" he asked, closing the space between us again. "Maybe you *don't* like "Reid Bennet for City Council", but that's... barely me. You *do* know me."

I huffed. "This is my first time seeing your face and knowing it's you! *Do I* know you?"

"Yes," he insisted, returning his hands to my waist, pulling my hips against his. "You know *this*. You know my thoughts, my feelings, my dreams. My failings." He lowered his head, brushing his lips against mine. "You know my touch... my heartbeat... my skin..." he pressed his mouth to mine, just gently at first before invading with his tongue, in a kiss that made me feel dizzy. "So... are you really going to act like you don't know me?"

I whimpered as he bent just enough to get his hands under the full skirt of my dress, hiking it up as he stood.

"Reid... I came here with Jeff... you're with your fiancée..."

"And neither one of us gives a damn about either of them... do we?" he asked, leaving my dress hiked around my hips as he quickly undid his pants.

I didn't answer.

Couldn't answer, because I was ashamed of my answer. But that didn't keep me from willingly hooking my legs around his waist as he lifted me up, or helping guide him into me as he pressed me into the wall. I was glad for the soft covering of the leaves over the brick as he drove into me – deep and fast, with urgent strokes that left me panting as I locked my arms around his neck as he kissed me.

124

That was urgent too.

Deep strokes with his dick and deep strokes with his tongue, both trying to convince me of... *something*. My mouth fell open as he buried his face in my neck, kissing me there as he burrowed into me as far as he could go, like he never wanted to leave.

And maybe that's what this was.

Him making his mark on me while he could, because once we left this party, there was really no telling what happened next.

I didn't want to think about what happened next.

I just wanted him, long and thick inside of me, fucking me like he'd never get another chance, hands gripping my ass as I slipped up and down over the ivy. I maneuvered my hands under his tuxedo jacket to dig my nails into his shoulders through his shirt as he slammed into me with purpose, using his knowledge of my body to send me rocketing to an orgasm that had me damn near biting a hole through my lip to keep from screaming.

He drove into me several more times before he came with a low growl, buried so deep that our hips were practically fused. We stayed like that for several moments, catching our breaths before he finally pulled out, and pulled away.

For a few more seconds, we just stared.

And then I remembered where I was.

Who *he* was.

And what was happening around us.

I hurriedly fixed my dress, and tried to fluff my hair, picking through it to make sure I was free of leaves. I glanced around on the ground, trying to figure out when and where I'd dropped my clutch while Reid calmly fixed his own clothes.

"Rowan," he said, and I ignored him as I reached to pick it up, pulling out a handkerchief to wipe the lipstick stain from my mouth before I had to find a bathroom and use it to clean other places. "*Rowan*," he insisted again, this time grabbing me and turning me to face him.

"What?" I snapped, angry all over again – partially at myself for what we'd just done, and the fact that it'd felt so dangerously good.

"I'm going to fix this. We're going to be together."

My eyes narrowed. "Are we, Reid? How do you propose we'll manage that?"

"I don't know, but... I give you my word. And I always keep my word. I want you, Rowan. And I have every intention of having you."

"Because I'm under contract, right?" I shook my head. "Would you really do that, at this point? Compel me to come to you, to be with you, based on that?"

Looking into his eyes, I could tell he was desperate. And honestly... part of me found it profoundly endearing, and romantic, but I realized that part of me was fucking stupid. Because that part of me was, somehow, enamored with this man, before I even knew who he was.

But now that I did... I recognized how insane it was.

"If that's what it takes to make my feelings clear to you... yes. Until our contract is over... I expect you to hold up your end."

I swallowed, hard. Simultaneously turned on and insulted.

"Fine," I whispered, looking away from him to grab the balcony door. "Just tell me what time to be there."

Shit.
Shit.
Shit.

126

I couldn't say I'd overplayed my hand, because I wasn't sure it was that – I wasn't sure I'd even been looking at my cards before I just threw them all on the table, strategy be damned.

I wanted Rowan

I didn't want the Grant family.

I didn't want the politics, at least not in the useless manner I'd been pursuing.

It was incredibly simple.

"*Who the fuck do you think you are*?!" Julius bellowed, *way* too close to my goddamn face, but I steeled myself, playing it cool. There was nothing to be gained by losing it – not right now, at least.

One way or another… this would come out like I wanted.

"I *know* that I am a grown man, who has grown tired of politics. The campaign didn't work, and I'm done with it. I'm conceding tomorrow, while I have some pride and reputation left. Enid can tell whatever lie she wants about our breakup, as long as it doesn't veer into attacking my integrity. Everybody wins."

Julius' light brown skin flushed red. "Everybody wins?! Do you know how much money I've sunk into your campaign little boy?! For you to sit here and tell me you're *quitting*, and dumping my daughter – before *my* election?!"

"I will write you a check for your trouble, *old man*. With interest. And we *will* call it square."

"You don't tell me what I'll do—"

"I'm pretty goddamn sure I just did," I snapped, tired of this conversation. I wasn't sure where I'd gone wrong – where I'd framed the shit as it if were a discussion, or a debate. It was a courtesy – one I was right on the line of rescinding.

"You don't know who you're messing with, boy," Julius warned, standing from his seat in front of my desk, where this conversation had been taking place. It was well after the gala, and I was tired, frustrated, and hungry.

For Rowan.

This bullshit was keeping me from handling what I considered to be a more pressing situation.

So, in the interest of getting it over with, I stood too, putting my hands in my pockets and looking Julius right in his face. "Neither do you, *pops*," I goaded, since he was still making digs at my age. "Let's just say… you aren't the only person I know with… a seat at a certain table. It's in your best interests to keep things civil… I promise you."

Julius' eyes narrowed in understanding, but behind him, Enid piped up, breaking her father's demand from the beginning of the conversation that she remain quiet.

"You might be untouchable, but your girlfriend isn't."

Despite the fact that my heart slammed to the front of my chest, I maintained my composure. "Excuse me?"

"Rowan Phillips, you son-of-a-bitch. It's all over the gossip blogs tonight."

Julius frowned, turning to her. "What is?"

"The way he looked at her tonight, when he was helping her with those cheap ass shoes! Do you know how embarrassing this is for me?! They're calling her fucking Cinderella!"

I stifled a laugh. "Sounds like you embarrassed *yourself* Enid. As usual. You're the one who spilled the drink, are you not?"

"And you couldn't wait to run and help her!"

"And Jeff Perry couldn't wait to run and help you, so you want to talk about *that*?"

She scoffed. "As long as you want to talk about him seeing you at the Drake hotel, sneaking around. Who were you meeting, Reid? Was it her?"

128

"Oh, so you and Jeff talk often? You fucking him too?"

"That's *enough*," Julius growled, making me grin. Of *course* he didn't want to hear about his daughter's dirt. "I don't give a shit about these affairs – you two had better not fuck up my campaign."

I shrugged. "I've got no such plans. But you may want to put a muzzle on your bi… *daughter*. I see she's good friends with Jeff Perry, has him checking up on me. If I see even a *hint* of my business in public… I'll bury the Grant name in so much bullshit you'll need a bulldozer to get out."

"Are you threatening me?"

"Nope," I shook my head. "I'm promising. But let's be clear – I don't want any trouble with you, Julius. I just want *out*. And I don't want my name in your daughter's mouth."

"It won't be," Julius said, shooting Enid a look that said he intended to make sure she fell in line.

"Then you and I are good. I'll concede tomorrow, and you'll still have my endorsement."

Julius nodded. "Then… I guess our business is done."

To my relief, he didn't try to shake hands or any of that – he just turned and left, and I honestly hoped it would be the last time I saw him.

"Enid," I called, as she turned to follow. "Your shit will be packed and delivered wherever you want it, but I want all traces of you out of my house by this time tomorrow."

She turned to meet my gaze with a glare.

"You may be able to punk my father with your little veiled threats, but you don't scare me. One itty bitty comment, and your charity case is done for."

I smirked. "I don't know what you think you know, Enid, but if you were smart, you'd be scared."

"I know plenty, Reid. I smelled that grotesque perfume when I bumped into her tonight – the same scent you've had on you after you've been with her. It's on you *now*. She went out to take a phone call – came back looking well fucked. Ten minutes later... so did you. You got sloppy tonight, Reid. If you want to play this game with me... you should be more careful."

Before either of us knew it, I was across the room, right in her face, sparking visible fear in her eyes, just like a few nights ago.

"So should you," I told her, giving her a wide smile that must have made her realize she needed to move her ass on.

Enid was a lot of things, but she wasn't stupid.

Once she was gone, I could finally breathe.

Finally *think*.

Finally do what I should have done in the first place, before I set the wheels of a potential disaster in motion, based on my volatile ass feelings.

Call Des.

And hope it wasn't too late to make this all work out the way I wanted.

Nine.

I couldn't stop staring at the phone.

Waiting, waiting, and waiting some more to get that text or phone call.

*Maybe all this time spent waiting, you could be deciding what you're going to do when he **does** call.*

Ah.

Yes.

There was *that*.

The fact that, twelve hours after cleaning the residue of our little balcony tryst from between my legs in a tiny bathroom stall, I had *no* idea how I was going to react to Reid. The next time I read his words, heard his voice… saw his face.

Logically, not much had changed now that I knew his name – the contract was still in place, I was still expected to fulfill my end of the bargain. But… we weren't dealing with logic anymore. We were somewhere in the realm of *completely crazy*, and for some ridiculous reason… I wasn't ready to get off the bus.

I shouldn't have read about him.

That had probably been my mistake.

When I was still disgusted with what little I knew of his politics, it was very easy to decide that I wanted nothing to do with *Reid Bennet for City Council*. The problem with that?

It wasn't who he always was.

As soon as I'd gotten home from the gala, I'd pulled open my laptop without even bothering to take off my dress. From my couch, I read every article, every mention, using the new information to add to the things he'd told me in confidence, while

I was wearing that mask. Together, they painted a picture of a man who'd overcome rough beginnings to become the man he was today – confident, conscious, compassionate, and on a mission to affect change in young people trying to navigate the same maze he'd already conquered.

A leader.

An intelligent, attractive, assertive one.

Who was great in bed.

A damned *dream*.

An *engaged* one.

I pushed out a sigh and reached for the remote, shaking my head as I thought about his claim from the night before.

"I'm going to fix this. We're going to be together."

I snorted.

Yeah, right.

He wasn't the first man to claim he was giving it all up, leaving the wealth and influence behind to be with their mistress.

It never happened.

And surely, it wasn't about to start now.

Despite my frustrations, I couldn't help the way my shoulders instantly perked up at the sight of Reid Bennet himself, on my TV. It was a live shot – it was archive footage from another time. But it was playing because, apparently, he had some sort of special campaign announcement about to happen.

Momentarily.

And I *definitely* had a moment.

Or at least, I thought I did, until a knock sounded at my door.

I glanced at the time, noting that it was barely nine in the morning before my face settled into a scowl. I'd already debriefed with Laurel, and she was busy today anyway, so I knew it wasn't her. Anyone else I knew, knew to call before they popped up at my place. So with that in mind, I naturally assumed it was someone who didn't feel bound to the normal laws of courtesy.

Desiree Byers.

Of course he sent her.

With a deep sigh, I flipped the TV off and tightened my robe around the nothing I had on underneath, so I could go answer the door. Instead of simply opening it, I stopped to look through the peephole, and was glad I did.

Des wasn't at the door.

Jeff Perry was.

Frowning, I looked down for another check of my appearance, making sure I was well covered before I opened the door.

"Jeff... what can I do for you?" I asked, noting the fact that he seemed a little subdued. "Is something wrong?"

"I wondered the same thing... can I come in?"

It was on the tip of my tongue to ask why, but after I'd screwed another man and then cut our "date" short the night before, I felt like a little amiability was in order. I stepped aside, welcoming him in and crossing my arms over my chest to make sure my nipples weren't being unruly after I'd closed the door.

"You seemed a little stressed when I left you last night," Jeff started, closing some of the distance I'd left between us. "Thought I'd check in on you. Did you get that issue worked out, with the center?"

Issue?

"Oh, uh.... Yeah. The doors and windows definitely *were* locked, so... no worries there."

Across from me, Jeff's eyes narrowed. "Oh. Uh... that's good. Wouldn't want anyone there who wasn't supposed to be."

"Right," I agreed. "Never can be too careful. Sorry that I was so distracted last night, thinking about it. I hope you aren't too upset about me having to cut things short."

He gave me an odd smile. "No, not at all. Just glad to see you up and about... getting some work done," he said, motioning toward my open laptop.

"Don't—"

Shit.

It was too late.

He'd already tipped the screen back, his eyes skimming quickly skimming over the multiple open tabs that still held mention after mention of Reid.

"Researching Reid Bennet, are you?"

Keeping my expression and voice neutral, I nodded. "Yes. He claimed to be considering a donation last night. I never looked into him very much after the softball game, but if he's giving money to the Cartwright Center, I figured it was probably best to know as much as possible."

"Oh," Jeff smirked. "And here I thought you already knew plenty."

My eyebrows went up. "Excuse me?"

"I think you're pretty clear on what I said, but let me make it plain – I saw the way you looked when you got back from "making a phone call". *Before* you hit the bathroom to fix yourself up. And I saw who came in after you, looking significantly... *lighter.*"

Goddamnit.

"Exactly what are you implying, Jeff?"

"I'm not implying *shit.* I'm telling you that I know you're fucking Reid Bennet – I'm just not one hundred percent yet on *why.* I'm leaning toward the money – things suddenly got *real* good at the center around the time of that softball game. Guess the kids weren't the only ones hitting home runs."

"Get the hell out of my apartment," I snapped, pointing toward the door as if he needed directions.

He raised his hands. "Hey, no offense intended. I can respect a nice hustle. This probably won't be your apartment very much longer, will it? Reid will want his mistress somewhere less accessible."

"You can kiss my ass!"

"Oooh, no exclusivity? Damn, I thought Bennet would be a little more selfish than that. As a matter of fact – I'm surprised he let you come out to the gala with me at all… but then again, you two wouldn't have been able to do your whole pretend-not-to-know-each-other role play bullshit if you hadn't. I'm *really* surprised you didn't meet up after. I waited around you know… catch him sneaking here, catch you sneaking out. Guess he was too busy with other things to reach out. Did he not even call?"

"Your ass has two seconds to get the fuck out of here," I snapped, grabbing my keys – and the pepper spray can attached to them – from the table beside the door. "Or you're gonna wish—"

My threat was interrupted by the chime I'd been waiting on all night and all morning – the notification that Reid was reaching out to me, via that exclusive cell phone. The problem? Jeff noticed how completely that sound snatched my attention, and *he* was closer to the phone sitting on my coffee table than I was.

He reached for the phone at the same time I dove at him.

I had no idea what I was thinking – I was naked under that flimsy robe and nowhere near a match in strength for Jeff. All I knew was that I wasn't about to let him see what Reid had sent me now that everything was in the open between us. There

135

was no telling what incriminating thing he might say, and no telling what Jeff might do with the information.

It was futile though.

Jeff easily reached the phone, and had it firmly in hand by the time I got to him, trying to snatch it away. We struggled with it for a few seconds before he put his full strength into shoving me backward, a move that sent me into a heap on the floor, half my body exposed in my tangled robe.

Above me, Jeff leered. "Nice goods, but I bet you everything I need is right here on this phone. Is this how he stays in touch?"

Without thinking, I lashed out, kicking him right in the shin. He immediately crumpled in pain, giving me enough time to push myself up, snatch that phone from his hand, and run in the opposite direction.

Not fast enough, though.

I screamed when I felt his arms around me from behind, snatching my feet off the ground as I struggled against him.

"Just give me the goddamn phone Rowan!" he hissed, grabbing my wrists to keep me from fighting. "We just want him – not you!"

"I'm not giving you *shit*!" I kicked backward with as much force as I could – not enough to do anything – but enough to make him shove me away from him again. This time, I went toppling forward, phone still in my hand as I flailed for something, anything, to grab.

There was nothing.

And after I hit the floor with a smack... there was even less.

"Come on, baby... pick up."

I frowned at my phone as the line I'd opened specifically for Rowan went to the unestablished voicemail box yet again. I'd already been on my way to her when I first started calling, hoping to at least give her a *little* warning before I just popped up.

But it seemed like the least I could do, after… everything.

But I had to see her.

I felt freer than I had since I first allowed myself to get wrapped up in Julius Grant's web. Since I first fell for the wolf in sheep's clothing that was his goddamn daughter. Enid was right about one thing – she *was* better at the trickery and lies – I'd truly cared for her, despite the fact that the shit was an act.

What Enid didn't understand though, was that I'd burn all this shit down without a second thought before I'd go out like a bitch and let her and father take this control shit too far.

Reputation be damned.

Career be damned.

Reid Bennet may be a lot of things, but controllable wasn't one of them. And I was done letting the Grants think I was, now that this situation was no longer favorable to me.

Which was exactly why I'd spent my morning delivering a succinct statement that I was – in better words – done with this shit.

No more campaign.

No more Enid.

No, I wasn't taking questions.

All I wanted was Rowan.

If she'd just pick up the damn phone.

I was in the car outside her apartment building now, growing impatient. Des had urged patience, to maybe give Rowan – and myself, honestly – a few days to decompress, and process everything, but again… all I wanted was her.

I was lifting the phone to my ear to call one last time when movement caught my attention. My eyes narrowed as I watched Jeff Perry emerge from the front door of Rowan's building, looking up and down the street like he was afraid of being seen, and then scurrying away to the parking lot. I watched, trying to figure out what the hell was going on, but it was clear when he went straight to a car I immediately recognized, barely getting the door closed before it peeled off.

Enid.

Fuck!

"Follow them, and call Des, immediately," I barked at Kerri, the security guard who was with me for the day, before I hopped out of the car. I trusted her to know exactly how to handle the situation, because as much as I wanted to run up on Jeff myself, it was more pressing for me to check in with Rowan.

Something was wrong.

My heart raced as I took the stairs two at a time instead of waiting for the elevator, bolting to Rowan's door as soon as I reached her floor. I knocked at first, frantic raps at the solid surface that went unanswered, and then, instead of knocking again… I tried the doorknob.

My heart dropped when it opened.

I saw her as soon as I was inside, sprawled out on the floor, her robe barely closed over her nude body. I dropped to my knees beside her, wanting to pull her into my lap but also afraid to touch her, afraid to make it worse. The knot on her head brought a fresh wave of rage over me, and I leaned over her, gently patting her face.

138

"Rowan. Rowan… *Rowan*, baby… wake up. What happened? What did he do to you?"

"Reid. Talk to me. What's going on?"

I damn near jumped out of my skin at the sound of Des' voice behind me – at first, I'd thought it was Rowan speaking.

"How the *fuck* did you get here so fast, and why are you sneaking up on me?"

She shook her head, all business as she stalked across the room on her heels. "I was already on my way – hall camera caught Jeff Perry going in, and I have his face flagged." She held up a finger to me while she tapped out a text to someone as she peered down at Rowan. "Good thing too, because he was obviously up to no good. Looks like there was a struggle. What's missing?"

I frowned. "I don't give a shit what's missing – I need to get her to a hospital."

"You don't want to answer hospital questions, Reid – not an hour after suspending your campaign. I already have it handled. My doctor is on the way."

"Loren?"

"Who else would it be?" she asked, impatient, then held up a hand again as she received a call. "Talk to me. Make it good news. Okay…. Okay… okay… good." She hung up, turning to me with a serious expression. "Our people got Jeff and Enid. They're holding them."

"Where?" I growled, already prepared to go kick ass until Des held a hand up.

"There's a problem. Jeff called the police. Anonymous tip, a woman screaming – he wants to make sure he doesn't end up with a murder charge. You have to go. *Now.*"

"And what are *you* going to do?"

She smirked. "What I always do, honey. Fix it. Now go."

139

I didn't want to leave Rowan, but I was very confident that Des really did have a handle on it. As soon as I reached the door to the apartment, her people were on me, leading me out of the building and out of sight just as the police pulled up, lights flashing.

While Des was taking care of Rowan… I was going to take care of Jeff.

I've come too far to go to prison now.
I've come too far to go to prison now.
I've come too far to go to prison now.

I kept telling myself that, but I wasn't sure how well the message was hitting home, because as soon as I saw Jeff, my first inclination was to punch him in his fucking face, and not stop. This was probably why Des had the two of them transferred to an empty room in her office suite, instead of somewhere I could peacefully commit a murder.

Always encouraging the goddamn high road.

I swiped a hand over my face and then stopped my pacing, entering the room with Kerri in tow – not by my request, and not for my protection, I was sure. At least, not for my physical protection against Enid or Jeff.

Protection against myself, against doing something I wouldn't regret, but wouldn't be smart either.

"Tell me what the fuck this is supposed to be," I demanded, looking back and forth between Jeff and Enid, neither of whom looked scared enough for my tastes. "You two working together or something? Some kinda fucked up dynamic duo?"

Enid – with the protection of a bodyguard between us – snorted. "Damn right. I told you not to underestimate me, Reid. You may have gotten in front of us this time, but this damn sure isn't over."

"It absolutely is – I guess ol' Perry over here didn't tell you he left Rowan Phillips on her floor naked with a concussion and a knot the size of a basketball on her head," I said, forcing the words through my teeth, because it pissed me off all over again just to think about it. "Sounds like assault charges and some other shit to me, and I bet between me and Des, we can make some accomplice charges happen for you. And your daddy can kiss that election goodbye."

I was right – Jeff must *not* have said anything to her about it yet, because her eyes went big as saucers and then the next thing I knew, she flew at him, scratching and clawing like she was trying to rip him open.

"I told you we needed *proof* asshole, and you assaulted her!? What the fuck is wrong with you?!" she screamed, fighting against the security guard that had pulled her off of him.

"So you admit the shit?" I said, shaking my head. "After I told your ass to leave her alone, and let it go, you just couldn't do it."

"Fuck her, and fuck *you!*" Enid sneered. "I hate you!"

"The feeling is *beyond* mutual, sweetheart. Now what am I gonna do with you? You obviously don't know how to quit while you're ahead, so I guess I have to stop making threats and just… do what I promised."

She scoffed. "You wouldn't *dare*. All you'll do is embarrass yourself in the process too."

I chuckled. "Nah, love. The difference between me and you? I don't care about this shit. So I got cheated on? Who gives a fuck. *You* lose. Your father loses. Your whole family loses. And there isn't shit you can do. Make sure you watch the news tonight."

For the first time, when the fear came into Enid's eyes, it stayed there as she pleaded. "Wait! Wait, fine. *Fine*, okay? I'll leave it alone. I'll let it go. But my father will kill me if—"

"I don't really give a fuck," I told her, looking her right in the face. "You're nothing to me. And... I thought I was nothing to you? *"Not that nigga"*, remember?"

"Reid, *please*. *Please!*" she shrieked, as I motioned for the security guard to take her out, leaving me with only Jeff, who looked like he'd been locked in a cage with a feral cat. I could still hear Enid pleading, as if I hadn't given her ass chance after chance, only to have it ignored.

Her fate was sealed, as far as I was concerned.

Jeff though... he'd put his hands on Rowan.

"You know I can't let this shit slide, right?" I asked, stepping in front of him. Kerri cleared her throat, warning me not to get to close.

"Reid... it was an accident. I was just trying to get the phone."

My eyes narrowed. *"Why?* Enid has you sprung like that?"

"No," he shook his head. "I just... I *need* this story. My cousin... Nubia... she's threatening to fire me from this position if I don't get my shit together."

"And *this* is together?"

"No! I just... I sniffed out that there was something going on between you and Rowan. Just a hunch. And I knew if I broke a story like that – the *real* reason for you ending your campaign, breaking up with Enid – I'd be undeniable."

I shook my head. "So nigga you're telling me you put Rowan's health at risk for a fucking *story?*"

142

"She wasn't supposed to get hurt! She shouldn't have fought, she should've just given me the goddamn ph—*Ahhh shit!*"

As soon as he opened his mouth to even *seem* like he was blaming her for this, I saw red all over again. Before I knew it, before I could stop myself, I'd popped him in his jaw, and was poised to do it again when Kerri pulled me back with a smirk.

"I let you have that one boss, but you know Des will blow her top if I give you another one."

I lifted my hands, conceding to her point because she was right – It was Des' job to keep my name out of trouble, and if I was out here kicking ass, it made her job harder. When I hired her though, it was with my political aspirations in mind. Aspirations that were the last thing I gave a fuck about right now, making it much easier to decide I cared more about him paying for whatever the hell he'd done to Rowan than I cared about a reputation.

Just as I made that decision, my phone rang – like Des was reading my mind.

"She's going to be fine," she told me, as soon as I picked up. "I want you here when the doc clears her for visitors. And I think she'd want you here too."

I shook my head. "In a little bit. I just need to take care of something first."

"Reid, all you need to take care of is the woman who has a massive headache after this morning's drama. You gonna do that from a jail cell?"

"So I'm supposed to just let this ride?!"

"You are *supposed* to prioritize," Des snapped. "According to Rowan, he pushed her – which still isn't okay by any means, but it's not as if you need to avenge a beating or something. *This* is not the thing you dirty your own hands with – especially not with violence."

"I hear what you're saying, but… I'm not trying to hear this shit."

"Then hear *this* – Rowan isn't the type of woman who is going to want a man who wields his fists as a weapon just because he can. You have better tools in your inventory. *Use them.* Be smart about this! If you let anger get in front of you, guess who suffers? Here's a hint – it isn't you, and it isn't goddamn *Jeff Perry.* It is *Rowan* – the woman at the center of this, who the media is going to drag through the dirt and discredit, ruining what she's worked for. Or did you think you were going to kick Jeff's ass and he was just going to shut up about it?"

"He assaulted her!"

"And a pissed off man in jail is still a man with a fucking story, Reid! *Be smart.*"

I suppressed a groan as I looked over at Jeff's bitch ass holding his jaw, looking like he was on the verge of tears between the pain I'd just inflicted and the situation he'd created for himself.

"Reid…," Des said, pulling my attention back to the phone. "When you called me last night, angry and confused, I asked you a question. Do you remember that?"

"Des…"

"I asked you what you wanted – what you *really* wanted," she continued, like I hadn't said anything. "And you told me that you wanted a life with Rowan – a life of service, and growth, with a woman who makes you want to be a better man. Is that *really* what you want?"

"It *is.*"

"Then fucking act like it! I'll take care of Jeff, and I'll take care of Enid. *You* come and be here for the woman you want."

I heard what Des was saying – really, I did.

And I recognized that she was right.

But neither of those things tamped down my desire to put Jeff's head through a wall when I thought about how I'd found Rowan on the ground.

How afraid had she been, alone in her apartment with this clown? What had gone through her mind when, instead of just giving up the phone – which was circumstantial evidence at best, and couldn't be tied directly to me, something Rowan probably didn't know – she'd risked her safety to protect my privacy?

And I was supposed to just... *leave*?

"I gotta go, Des," I told her, ignoring her shrill admonitions as I pulled the phone from my ear and hit the button to end the call.

It was time for Jeff and I to come to an understanding.

I definitely need something stronger than whatever the hell she gave me.

I kept my eyes closed, letting the hot water from the shower run over me as I tried to will away the throbbing pain in my head. This morning had been a mess – the run-in with Jeff, waking up to Des in my face, and then paramedics, and then the private doctor who'd shown up at Des' request.

All because of Reid, who I hadn't even seen yet.

I knew he'd dropped out of the campaign.

I knew he'd publicly ended things with Enid.

I knew he'd tried to call. What I didn't know was where he was now, while I was in pain and wondering what the hell was going on.

After a few more minutes, I turned the shower off, wrapping myself in the warm, thick robe that was waiting on a hook outside the door. I peered at myself in the fancy non-fogging mirror, cringing at the raised bruise that covered a good part of my forehead.

A glass of wine would be *so* good right now.

Des had insisted on checking me into a hotel, for both comfort and privacy. Of course she'd chosen the Drake, but we weren't in Reid's suite. It was a lush, small room – the perfect size just for me… or so I thought.

When I stepped out of the bathroom, I found Reid seated at the end of the bed, head in his hands. He looked up as a soft sound of surprise spilled from my throat, and then immediately stood.

"How are you feeling?" he asked, but kept his distance, shoving his hands into his pockets like it was the only way he could keep them to himself.

"Like shit. Are you here to collect on our contract anyway?"

I knew it was a low blow, but didn't stop myself from saying it. I was still confused, still frustrated, still… angry.

Or at least, wanted to be.

The sincere contrition in his eyes as he took a few steps toward me melted my ire away.

"I think you know the answer to that already," he said, cautiously taking my hand as he got a little closer, enough to

146

brush his lips against my temple as he changed his mind about holding hands, and wrapped me in his arms. "I'm sorry this happened."

"Yeah. Me too." I took a deep breath in, inhaling the warm scent of his cologne. "What now?"

He pulled back, to look me in the eyes. "For us?"

"For *you*. Assuming you aren't going to be arrested over Jeff."

She didn't know it, but I'd overheard the conversation when Des had called Reid to let him know I was okay.

Hours ago.

Of course I didn't know what Reid had said to her, but I knew Des had practically begged Reid not to give in to violence, citing my certain displeasure if he did. Whatever he'd said, it had her worried, calling other people to make sure Reid didn't do anything crazy.

I hoped he hadn't done anything crazy.

"Do you *want* me to get arrested over Jeff?" he asked, earnestly, which made me laugh. "Because you say the word, and I'll get at him."

"*No*. I want you to let Des handle it. That's what she's good at, right?"

"It is. But still."

"It's fine."

"You have a knot on your head."

"And I have *you* here."

Both of our eyes went wide over words I hadn't even meant to say out loud – hell, words I didn't even know were in me. But the cocky little grin that spread over Reid's lips made it worth it.

"So what are you saying?" he asked. "Last night… it didn't seem like you wanted much to do with me."

I shrugged. "Because I *didn't* want much to do with *Reid Bennet For City Council*, engaged to Enid Grant, protégé of Julius Grant. But Nick Bennet from the hood, who used to bang a little, but never got caught, who cleaned up his act and uses philanthropy to reach and help the kids from his ward, who questions the political process but wants to be a force for good... *that* guy... I'm interested in seeing what could happen with him."

"Meaning... the position is mine?"

"Meaning you're welcome to apply, and your application will be considered. Strongly considered, since I know you're good with your hands."

He grinned. "That is a challenge I gladly accept, Ms. Phillips. Can I get an application for a job too, while we're at it?"

I raised an eyebrow. "Seriously? At the Cartwright Center?"

"Yeah, why not? I can't just sit around and do nothing, right? And what better way to learn about actually impacting my community than from someone who is actually about it, versus talking about it."

"I mean... I think it's great, I just assumed you'd want to lay low for a bit... until after this stuff with Enid, and Jeff has blown over. Not to mention, you *just* canceled your campaign."

"I want to hit the ground running – and Jeff and Enid are already taken care of. Des' way. She now has a future Congressman who owes her a *huge* favor, and one of the biggest news sources in the state at her fingertips. Leverage. Invaluable."

I nodded. "Smart woman. I like it."

"I don't," Reid admitted. "But if it's good with you, I guess... it's good with me."

"Then we're good."

"Enough about that," he said, pulling me closer to him. "What about you? Des and the doctor said you were fine, but my eyes are telling me something else with this knot."

"I'm fine, Reid. Just a headache and a little bump. Nothing that sleep won't cure."

Reid frowned. "But you aren't supposed to sleep, are you?"

"No," I sighed. "So I guess I have to figure out another way to relax…" the look on my face must've helped him catch the hint, because his eyebrows went up.

"You're serious?"

"I am," I nodded. "Make me cum. Right here, in this room, in this bed. Lights on. No mask. Just me and you. And then… lunch. In this bed. No mask. Just me and you. And then make me cum again. You think you could work that out for me, or is it asking too much?"

He smiled, and shook his head.

"Not at all. Sounds like our initial arrangement – mutually beneficial."

-the end.

Christina C. Jones is a modern romance novelist who has penned many love stories. She has earned a reputation as a storyteller who seamlessly weaves the complexities of modern life into captivating tales of black romance.

Other titles by Christina Jones
Love and Other Things
Haunted (paranormal)
Mine Tonight (erotica)
Equilibrium
Love Notes
Five Start Enterprises
Anonymous Acts
More Than a Hashtag
Relationship Goals
High Stakes
Ante Up
King of Hearts
Deuces Wild
Sweet Heat
Hints of Spice (Highlight Reel spinoff)
A Dash of Heat
A Touch of Sugar
Truth, Lies, and Consequences

Inevitable Seductions
The Wright Brothers:
Getting Schooled – *Jason & Reese*
Pulling Doubles – *Joseph & Devyn*
Bending The Rules – *Justin & Toni*
Connecticut Kings:
CK #1 Love in the Red Zone – Love Belvin
CK #2 Love on the Highlight Reel
CK #3 – Determining Possession
CK #4 – End Zone Love – Love Belvin

Made in the USA
Middletown, DE
09 June 2023